THE BUTTON AND THE BOOK

A Novel

Narcisa Vucina

Translated from the original Danish by
Sinéad Quirke Køngerskov

SPUYTEN DUYVIL

NEW YORK CITY

The novel is based on actual events, the characters are fictitious.

Special thanks to The Danish Arts Foundation for financial support towards the translation and publication of this book.

©2018 Narcisa Vucina
ISBN 978-1-963908-20-6
Published as *Tildas Hemmelige Bog* by Forlaget Hovedland
Translation © 2024 Sinéad Quirke Køngerskov
Cover photo © Milana Jovanov via Unsplash

1
THE HERB WOMAN
SARAJEVO, 1952–1959

She was called the "herb woman," but her granddaughter, my best friend, Flora, and I called her Tilda. Her ancestors had fled Spain in the fifteenth century and had settled in Sarajevo.

Tilda never talked about her husband, Moise. He died in the Buchenwald concentration camp and left behind a pocket watch and an article from the *New York Times*. She stored the article carefully in a wooden box on the writing bureau in the living room next to Moise's picture. The article mentioned one of his fellow students, Milan Šufflay, who during the dictatorship of the "Kingdom of Serbs, Croats, and Slovenians," was murdered in Zagreb in the early 1930s. Intellectuals from several countries protested fiercely, and Albert Einstein and others condemned the regime on the front pages of a newspaper.

Flora and I asked Tilda if she was sad that Moise wasn't alive, to which she replied, "You shouldn't be sad and angry for long. You could be attacked by evil spirits."

In Sarajevo, five families shared a three-story house with a large garden and teahouse in the middle of hilly terrain with grass, wildflowers, and fruit trees. The families, who were of different religions and nationalities, invited each other to their religious holidays, but most attended neither church, mosque, nor synagogue.

When Flora's family celebrated the Jewish Pesach, Tilda told them about the Sarajevo Haggadah, a sacred illuminated manuscript detailing the Jews' flight from Egypt. The book was smuggled out of Spain hundreds of years before when the Jews were forced to leave the country. At the end of the nineteenth century, it was sold to the National Museum in Sarajevo. Tilda had seen a copy of the sacred book and had been quite taken with its beauty. She couldn't forget the extraordinary illustrations.

Tilda had decorated the table for Easter with little bowls filled with herbs, fruit purée, hard-boiled eggs, and matza, unleavened flat bread. We children had to save one half of the bread. If the adults didn't find it, we got money. It was about hiding it in a good place. The most-used hiding places were closets and drawers. Once, I hid my half in my chair, but when I sat down without thinking, the bread broke, and when I got up again, crumbs fell on the floor in all directions. The guests looked at me reproachfully, but Tilda couldn't keep a straight face and burst out into a loud laugh.

When the guests had consumed copious amounts of wine and pear liqueur, they sang old love songs.

Tilda's favorite plant was rue. She pickled it with honey and stored it in jars. On the white labels she wrote the plant's Latin name: *Ruta graveolens*.

She mixed the strongly scented rue with cloves, coffee, lemon, and calendula and placed it all in a handmade cardboard box, which she opened when Sabbath came to a close. "There must always be rue in the mix," she said. "It holds your good destiny."

People from the most remote parts of Yugoslavia came to Tilda to be healed. Once, a farmer with pneumonia, maybe even lung cancer, turned up. He looked like he was at death's door. Tilda asked him to take off his shirt and lie down on the couch, after which she attached heated glasses to his chest. After a while, the heat reached his head. Startled, the farmer stood up and shouted as if in a frenzy, "I want a hen!"

Satisfied, Tilda announced the treatment had worked, and he could go home.

In the winter I was often plagued by swollen tonsils, and the family doctor stuffed me full of penicillin. It helped for a while, but the pain always came back and my tonsils always swelled again. I couldn't swallow and had to stay in bed. My mother ended up sending me down to Tilda, who gave me a glass of warm water with apple cider vinegar to rinse my throat with as she said encouragingly, "Vinegar softens the tonsils."

I had to drink the concoction seven times a day for three days. It tasted disgusting, and I was reluctant to take it, but my mother forced the hot vinegar down my throat, and after three days the swelling subsided and the pain was gone.

Once I hid behind the curtains to observe a ritual Tilda called, "Liberation from fear." This time it was Flora who was to be liberated.

Tilda took a spoonful of lead shot and held it over the fire until the shot melted. Then she covered Flora's face with a white sheet, poured two glasses of water, a spoonful of salt, a piece of bread, and a bunch of rue in a basin. Finally she added the melted lead. The water began to bubble and boil, and soon afterward there was a bang. Flora's head began to shake under the sheet, and unfazed, Tilda began to mutter:

"… *All fear and curses be chased away to a lonely place, to an uninhabited land, where roosters do not crow, where birds do not fly, where dogs do not bark … I have taken it from you and cast it to the devil …*"

Tilda pulled the sheet away from Flora's pale face. Flora had to taste a drop of the basin's contents with her index finger. Then she had to spit three times into the mixture while her grandmother chanted on.

"… *Three as a girl, three as a married woman, three as a widow, three as a divorced woman … Let it disappear deep into the sea, and I will give you something in return for the fever, the fear, for all kinds of diseases that have dwelt in this body … Let them all disappear into the depths.*"

Flora's face turned chalky white. Lead figures that looked like little devils jumped in the basin. When the figures had stopped moving, Tilda began to interpret them to learn where the fear was coming from. Her face lit up, and she ended the session with a series of blessings.

The lead cure was over, and Flora's face returned to its normal color.

***

The men talked about politics, the women about food and supernatural phenomena. Occasionally the women interrupted the men with "important" remarks. They intuitively knew which politicians were the "good" ones and how to cope with the latest cuts in food and transport.

When they didn't want to talk anymore, they laughed at the latest jokes. Afterward, they sang everything from melancholic folk songs to American pop songs. Someone suggesting Paul Anka's "Diana" or another popular folk song was enough to get them started.

Flora's mother pulled out her accordion and played the black and white keys. The faces of the singers shone with contentment as if the instrument's tones had awoken a forgotten love in their hearts. They got up and began to dance. They danced fast and frantically, stomping their feet to off-beat dance rhythms.

When the gramophone played Elvis Presley, their bodies entered a trance-like state, swaying back and forth on all sides, up and down, up and down. The high notes and rhythmical dance steps made Moise's gold-framed picture on the writing bureau shake.

But when Tilda started singing old Sephardic songs, silence fell. She knew them in Ladino and always ended with the song "Adio Kerida," Farewell My Love.

Tu madre kuando te parjo
I te kito al mundo
Korason eja no te djo
Para amar segundo.

Adio,
Adio kerida, no kero la vida
Me la margates tu …

(When your mother gave birth to you)
and took the world from you,
she didn't give you a heart
so you could love someone else.

Farewell,
Farewell my love.
I don't care for life
you have made it bitter.

Away and find another lover,
knock on someone else's door,
wait for someone else's ember,
to me you are dead.

Farewell,
Farewell my love.
I don't care for life
you have made it bitter.

***

Tilda died one day in 1958.

When her body was carried out of the house, I grew afraid of the unknown and mysterious world that awaited her on the other side of the clouds.

The adults said now there was no longer anyone who could help them with their illnesses and who could sing Sephardic songs.

Flora and I said there was no longer anyone who could teach us wise words, even if we didn't really know what they meant. The last phrase she taught us slipped out of our mouths in unison, like an ancient prayer. "Let our free will, and not fate, rule our lives."

2
THE SECRET BOOK
SARAJEVO, 1962

One day in June, fifteen years old, I was walking down the avenue by the Miljacka river, intoxicated by the scent of lime blossom and the gypsy music from a garden restaurant. Ladies in flowery dresses with necklaces and rings of gold ate and listened to the music with men in dark blue suits, white shirts, and ties. The ladies dried tears from their eyes, and the bells from the cathedral drowned out the breeze. It was a hot day. I remember it because of the lime blossom, the smell of food, and the longing for the music of a bygone era.

That was the day Flora was told she suffered from epilepsy. We sat silently on the bed in her parents' bedroom. The large, yellow quinces that lay on the closet pushed out the summer heat, spreading their fragrance despite having been picked a long time ago.

Flora got up from the bed and started pacing back and forth, then stopped abruptly, went to a dresser by the window, opened one of the drawers, and grabbed a neatly wrapped book, which she handed to me, saying, "This is Tilda's secret book. It's very valuable. She wanted me to have it, but now I'm giving it to you because I don't know how long I'm going to live. You have to take good care of it. The book holds several secrets. But you must promise me you won't open it before I'm dead."

3
NIKO
SARAJEVO, 1964

I stand looking out into the cloudy late summer morning behind the linden and chestnut trees whose yellow and orange foliage hangs low over the *Marshal Tito Barracks*. Sparrows sweep across the square, dipping their wings and the upper part of their breasts in the shiny puddles and flying away from the quivering water surfaces, chirping.

It has been raining continuously for two days, but this September morning the dark clouds lie hidden behind the horizon to let the white sun reveal itself as if it were performing a show for the heavens. There's a chill in the air. It smells of coal.

The mist disappears from fear of the sun. The morning is now quite bright. Clear and peaceful.

I stand outside the barracks, waiting for Niko. The last Saturday. In six days he will leave the barracks without his military uniform. I will miss the uniform. I miss it already.

The soldiers come out of the main door, out of the iron gate, all smelling of the same aftershave. They smile and quickly disappear along the dusty path that faces the street.

They can't see me looking at them. No one notices me staring at the point between their legs. I choose one with two powerful bulges in his crotch and imagine how we flee into the park on the other side of the street behind the National Museum where we are pushed against each other and swallowed by boiling blood and sour-smelling sweat. I undress him, fling his uniform into the hedge, and we throw ourselves down on the grass next to the rose bushes without letting go of each other … a squeal from my throat. He closes my mouth and whispers how much I mean to him. His hand is firm.

They need love, the soldiers, after the strenuous drills. They are strong, invincible, and ready to defend the country. I'm not afraid of anything at all. I know they look after me. Day and night. They are a warning to foreign powers that want to invade and occupy our homeland. Our soldiers. The Yugoslav People's Army.

At night I wait by the window for the young men

who have been called up for the army to sing their songs, happily drunk. The next day I sneak a peek as they walk along the street freshly shaved and barbered. I follow them on their way to the train station. A train is waiting there. The young men stand tall, full of expectations for a life in uniform. They sing the same song.

Comrade Tito, we swear we will never deviate from your path ...

***

The voice on the radio this morning sounded like Frank Sinatra's. Can't get the tune out of my head:

When I was seventeen
It was a very good year
It was a very good year ...

I can't remember any more lyrics. I feel like I'm starting to fear getting old, even though I'm only seventeen. I want to stay seventeen for a long time.

Last night my father and I argued over what we should listen to on the radio. I wanted Radio Luxemburg, he wanted *Glas Amerike*, "The Voice of America," an

American station that broadcasts news for Yugoslavs. After shouts, frowns, and threats, he won. I didn't get to hear The Shadows, who I'd been looking forward to hearing all day. He claimed it was very important for him to hear the news and that I had to do my homework anyway. He also said he wouldn't give me the money for the cinema if I didn't get good grades in my final exam at business school.

My father is easily irritated, even by little things. He has been like that since John F. Kennedy was assassinated last year. My mom, my brother, and I have been listening to stories about the Kennedy family for years. We even know the Irish village John's poor ancestors fled to America from, where, as my father pointed out, they fought their way to the top of politics with diligence and cunning, fulfilling the American dream.

My mom thinks my father looks like JFK, and a little like his brother, Robert, too, and one of my aunts thinks my father looks most like their brother, Teddy. My father says my mom looks like Elizabeth Taylor. Just without Elizabeth's eye color. Every year, on my mother's birthday, he gets her a poster, a black-and-white portrait of the actress from one of her films. Initially my mom hung the posters on the wall in the kitchen, but there's no more space now, so she has started hanging them in the living room and in the hallway.

She copies the dresses, skirts, and blouses "Beth" wears, sewing the clothes herself and donning them when we go to visit and when she goes to PTA meetings at the school. My mother's face lights up when other women admire her clothes, and men turn to look at her.

But she regrets only working in her profession for a few years, and she is afraid I will end up a stay-at-home mom like her. She wants me to be independent. I just haven't figured out what the word *independent* means yet. It reminds me of the words *brotherhood* and *unity* that we learned in school and that the politicians repeat again and again in their speeches.

For the past three years, my father and mom have been saving up for a trip to Italy to buy clothes and an accordion for my brother. Italian clothes are cheaper and better than Yugoslav ones. And more modern too.

Every other week, overcrowded buses run for a day and a half to Trieste and Venice where passengers find the cheapest markets to buy *šuškavac*, "rustling," thin, fluttering raincoats that crackle, high-heeled ladies' shoes, Levi's or Wrangler jeans, dolls, and crystal glasses and vases.

My brother got his accordion, and I got a winter coat. But now he doesn't want to play the accordion anymore. He's too busy reading books on weapons. On pistols and tanks, on machine guns and bombs. My mom blames my father, who got him the books. But my father believes that this way the "boy" will gain insight into the technological skills on which the new nuclear weapons era is based.

After the war, my father was nervous about Yugoslavia coming under Stalin. He certainly didn't want to live under the Russians. To him, they were still unpredictable and dangerous. But my mom considered the Russians our Slavic brothers, and she thought it was good they helped free Europe from the Nazis. By way of thanks, she gave me a Russian name—Masha. And she insisted on writing in Cyrillic letters, even though she was not a Serb, but a Muslim. Mind you, in those days, you couldn't tell the difference. My father, however, decided my brother was to have an American name, so his name is Robert. After Robert Kennedy.

My father's mother was Jewish and from Odessa,

Russia. Due to the persecution of Jews in 1905, her parents and siblings fled to Vojvodina. In the town of Zemun, the family opened a business selling dried cod, oat bread, and honey cakes. My grandmother met my grandfather at a market in the town where he was doing military service after World War I. Love at first sight, they knew their lives were to be intertwined. But her parents were against her marrying someone who was not of the Jewish faith. So my grandmother waited until my grandfather finished his military service, after which they fled to his village in Herzegovina. But she still had to become Catholic to marry him.

I haven't been in the village since my grandmother died four years ago.

Every summer vacation, my brother and I used to be sent by bus to visit her. The family in the village said I resembled her, not only in appearance but also in temperament. I found it flattering. She taught me how to listen to the wind and how to talk to horses. In the evenings, we would sit beside each other on a bench and look at the stars. She pointed to the zodiac constellations and spoke of Venus and other planets. As if what happened far away from us was part of her life on earth.

She smiled easily, and when she found things hard would say that *the planet Uranus brought unrest to her mind.*

Occasionally she longed for the time in Odessa, the smells of her childhood, the voices and songs of the synagogue. She still found it hard to understand how her life could have changed so much after finding love and said, "*It must have been fate.*"

***

Before my brother Robert and I went to bed last night, my mother came in and said she wanted to share a family secret with us. She spoke annoyingly slowly as the rain beat against the windowpanes and the sky glowed dark red with lightning. We needed to know the truth, she said, if something happened. Was she seriously ill? She wasn't, so I thought she was going to tell us another story about fighting during World War II, when she and my father, as partisans, attacked the Germans. But instead she told us about something that happened hundreds of years ago! What does it matter to me? I thought, but she had already begun the story. "My mother's family came from a people who called themselves the Bogomils. They lived in Bosnia in the Middle Ages. They had kings and their own church, and they were persecuted. And when the Ottomans conquered Bosnia-Herzegovina in the sixteenth century, many Bogomils converted to Islam."

My mother had heard the story from my grandmother, and my grandmother heard it from my great-grandmother who heard it from my great-great-grandmother. And now my brother and I were tasked with remembering it, my mother said solemnly. The weight of its responsibility seemed to fall on Robert and me now. We must now pass on the "secret." *To whom? I didn't even know if I wanted children. And if I had children, I was most likely not going to tell them this pointless story!*

***

At half past nine, Niko still hadn't shown up. Maybe he didn't have today off. I thought about how surprised he'd be when he saw me. At that moment Niko appeared in the main door of the barracks, looking out toward the park. He looked like Montgomery Clift in that movie where he played a soldier. Strange I hadn't thought of the similarity before. Except Niko didn't have Montgomery's enigmatic eyes. Niko's eyes were bright with a cheeky twinkle.

I started when I heard his voice. "Masha, has something happened?"

"Nothing. I was just thinking about how you would look out of uniform. Stop biting my neck, you horny idiot! My father was very interested to know where the bruises came from, so I had to lie to him. I can't stand living at home anymore. He listens to the news all the time!"

Niko could hardly wait until I'd finished talking. "Have you told them about our plan?"

"Only my mom. I dare not tell my father. He'll be furious. I haven't finished school. But I want to go with you, I can't be without you and your … but I can't handle their bickering either. Ten minutes later everything's all right again, and my father calls my mom his darling and gives her coffee and cake."

"You should be happy that your mother and father talk to each other. My parents barely speak to each other anymore. They use me as an intermediary. I've been trying to find out why they've fallen out. I think it's money. My father hasn't had a raise in years. He works from six in the morning until six in the evening. Last year, he almost died when he had to test new weapons.

The country needs to be prepared to defend itself against the enemy, and we don't know who that is. It's as if our leaders are still afraid of the Russians. And my mom, she works like crazy at home—washing clothes by hand, going to the market to buy cheap vegetables, tidying up, sweeping floors, polishing windows, standing by the oven. I'm not even sure if you could call it food. Flour dumplings, carrot soup, bread with pork fat sprinkled with sugar, cabbage, sauerkraut. And yes, a half a pound of ground beef for five people every three months. Dessert is rice pudding or cocoa with sugar and water. I don't understand why they don't help each other. Lots of other people are going through a hard time too. It's difficult to imagine they were once in love. I don't care, I'm going to make good money. I intend to send money home once a month when I start working. Hope you don't mind."

"Not in the slightest. But, there's something I have to tell you. I'm being followed."

"Followed by whom?"

"By a thought …"

"Tell me what it is."

"A weird feeling that something terrible is going to happen to Sarajevo. I can't explain it. I just feel like I have to get out of here. I see people suffering everywhere. In streets, in stairwells, at markets."

Niko didn't understand what I was talking about. Instead he asked if I had found a place where we could make love.

I said we could go to Flora's.

"She threw her mother and father out because she has to practice the piano. We can use their bedroom but only for an hour. Afterward, we can go to the cinema. Kino Partisan cinema is showing a new film. It's about a man who howls like a wolf and makes women go crazy, sexually."

The mahogany double bed that Tilda bought on installments in the late 1930s from the city's largest furniture store creaked so noisily Niko almost gave up touching me. Still, he asked if I'd brought a condom. I replied I hadn't and suggested he could come on my stomach. "I can't get pregnant right now. I'm not ovulating."

"You can't be sure of that. Surprises happen."

"I'm good at math."

Niko ejaculated his acidic liquid, and I felt something warm and slippery on my abdomen, from where it dripped down onto my thighs.

On top of the closet, on the other side of the double

bed, yellow, pear-shaped quinces flickered like flames with grayish tomentum, sending a raw, newly plucked, and intrusive scent of lemon and cardamom up my nostrils. The sweet-sour fragrance of the quinces was stronger than the sulfurous smell of Niko's seed. The sourness and the sweetness became one and the same smell.

I thought of Aphrodite, the Greek goddess of love, and ancient weddings where the bride was surrounded by quinces supposed to bring her fertility.

In our garden, the quinces from the old quince tree were plucked and diced every fall. Flora's mother and my mother would stand in the kitchen singing and making jelly. When the fruits hung on the branches with their fluff and steel-green matted leaves, they hid their fragrance and exhibited their hardness. But in winter, when the tree revealed its crooked branches that stretched out to the sides like tentacles, it frightened us children. Tilda used to say that when the trees were bare, they harbored ghosts. That was why Flora and I never went near the tree from December to March.

Niko turned his slender body on his side, laid his sweaty hand on mine, and asked, "What are you holding in your hand?"

"Something I hold dear."

"Can I see it? Show me," he said insistently, and with both hands, he began to open my hand. I couldn't resist his strength. A metal button with a red star in the middle fell out of my hand and rolled onto the sheet.

Niko stared at it and asked what I was up to.

I smiled. "I cut it from your uniform. I want a memory of you as a soldier."

I got up and went into the bathroom, scraped Niko's sperm from my stomach and stored it in a glass jar as a fortune teller had told Flora to do. The jar was to be handed over to the fortune teller who would utter some magic words, and then Niko and I would be together until death did us part.

***

Conscription lasted six months for the highly educated. Immediately after Niko was sent home, he was offered a job at a hospital in Dubrovnik, Croatia. He had completed his medical studies on time, graduated as a doctor when he was twenty-four and a surgeon when he turned twenty-nine. He couldn't get a job in Sarajevo. There were many applicants. Those who had connections were hired first.

We agreed I would move with him and do my last year of school in Dubrovnik. But my parents wouldn't hear of it. If I wanted to go with him, we had to get engaged first. And if we got engaged, we weren't allowed to live together before we wed, before I finished school, and turned eighteen. Until then, I was to live with my mom's friend, Emma.

I was surprised my mom and father were so conservative. I definitely hadn't imagined my mom would react like that. "As if I can't take care of myself. What is she thinking? She has always preached independence and women's liberation, but when her own daughter wants to stand on her own two feet, she can't figure out how to live up to her views."

Niko didn't think it was the end of the world. "They just want to show you mean a lot to them. And they are also worried about what family and friends will say when they hear their daughter, who has not yet turned eighteen, is living with a man she isn't married to. We live in a progressive society, but there are limits to how far we will go when it comes to family. Certain norms and traditions still live on … and I've noticed that you sometimes dramatize things, my dear. Calm down. It will all work out in the end. I didn't say I don't want to get married, did I? In fact, it suits me just fine to have a wife now that I have a job."

Niko smiled, pulled me into his arms, and whispered, "We could get married next summer. Then you will be of age and have finished school. I'm so looking forward to having you by my side."

4
PABLO
DUBROVNIK, 1965

A group of businessmen occupied almost all the tables in the restaurant where my mother's friend Emma had invited her daughter, Lina, and me out for dinner. A waiter appeared to lead us to an empty table by a large window on the west side where we could look out over the sea as the gulls flew with their silver wings toward the sun.

Emma taught biology at a high school, and now that I was living with them, she was helping me with my homework. I needed to get good grades on my final exams, she said, otherwise I would have no chance of finding a job. To make a good impression, I had to put up with her endless stories about how she made the pupils sit still and follow along during lessons. I involuntarily learned the most peculiar phenomena within biology, which has never interested me.

We just managed to place our order before Emma started to entertain us with how she taught ovulation and periods. Fortunately the waiter swiftly served a large platter of appetizers of cheeses, olives, and tomatoes as he said with a smile, "I am to say hello from your daughter's admirer."

Lina was flattered.

But when the waiter brought the main course, he handed a bouquet of flowers to me and said, "They're from your admirer."

I sat with my back to the "flower man." Didn't dare turn around, so I asked Lina what he looked like. She said he had large blue-green eyes, dark hair, long thick eyelashes, and a look that would instantly undress any woman.

The man got up, turned toward us elegantly, and introduced himself. "My name is Pablo Morena. I'm from Chile and work as an engineer at an aluminum factory. I was invited here to help rebuild Yugoslavia. But I get bored when I have time off. What about you?" he asked, looking at me. "How do you relax?"

"In bed," I answered promptly.

"I hope your boyfriend relaxes that way too."

"How do you know I have a boyfriend?"

"That's not hard. You're beautiful and remarkably intelligent. You probably have many admirers. But I don't think you've found the one yet."

"Are you implying something?"

"Maybe. You can try me."

"Try you! Like a car? And how does one try you, might I ask?"

"By saying yes to dinner."

"And you promise it's just dinner."

"Yes. The rest is up to you."

"Sounds very easy. Are all Chileans as direct and stubborn as you are?"

"I have no idea. I can only speak for myself. So, what do you say? Shall we have dinner tomorrow?"

I replied I couldn't tomorrow, but I could the day after, so we agreed to meet in a discreet place. He knew a restaurant with a garden on the outskirts of the old town.

***

When I entered the restaurant, Pablo was nibbling on delicate bites of feta cheese and olives and washing them down with red wine.

"I thought you weren't coming," he said as I took my chair.

"I waited ages for the tram," I replied, roused by his handsome appearance. I didn't really know how to continue, but words tumbled out of my mouth. "I wasn't sure if I should meet you. You probably have a wife and children at home in Santiago and just want to use me as a distraction."

"Do I seem like a married man who just wants a mistress?"

"You never know. People say so many things that have no basis in reality. To get girls."

"Shall I call my mother? Then you can ask her. And just to be clear, I'm not interested in mistresses. They're too complicated. I'm looking for a companion for life."

"A companion for life! Where do you find someone like that? You sound old-fashioned."

"Perhaps, but I only want the real deal."

"What do you mean by that?"

"I am faithful, and I want a faithful woman. In return, she will get everything she needs."

"How can you know you will be faithful all your life? Temptation is everywhere. Are you religious?"

"No. I'm an atheist. Well, a socialist. It is a question of morality, consideration for others, and trusting ..."

Pablo didn't get to finish the sentence because a waiter appeared with a pad and fountain pen to take our order. After carefully noting the desired dishes, he disappeared to the kitchen whereupon Pablo took out a small box wrapped in gold paper and handed it to me. "This is for you. You are welcome to see what it is."

I unwrapped the box and opened the lid.

"A ring?" I exclaimed. "I can't accept that. That's something you give to the person you are going to marry."

Pablo smiled. "After I saw you in the restaurant the day before yesterday, I said to my friend, 'I'm going to marry her, and our first son will be called Alberto.'"

"Romantic nonsense. I don't know you. I don't know who you are or what you want. Besides, I'm marrying my fiancé in three weeks."

An enormous moon above us shone on ripe bunches of grapes that hung heavily over multi-stemmed hibiscus bushes while the waves outside the restaurant's garden whispered words in an incomprehensible language.

***

Pablo led me into his dining room whose high and wide mosaic windows on the other side of the wall reflected the vibrant multi-colored light. Outside, in the distance, the sun kissed the sea and the yellowish light pressed through the windows as if the sun were hunting for love. The church bells chimed, but they couldn't drown out Pablo's voice. "I knew you'd come," he said. "My intuition never fails. I'm so glad you're here!"

There was a quiet beauty to Pablo and at the same time a particular unruliness. He was wearing a tulip-yellow short-sleeved shirt that revealed his strong arm muscles and taut stomach. His face turned pale in the whitewashed room, standing there surrounded by large Greek vases filled with fresh dark-red roses from the garden and looking like the Colossus of Rhodes. Untouchable, majestic, as though sent forth by Zeus himself. His deep voice sounded confident and polite as we strolled back and forth on a large Aubusson carpet with rose motifs. Gradually the fragrance of the roses was drowned out by a smell from the kitchen of roast lamb, lemon, and baked potatoes with rosemary. Pablo cast a kind look at me, our eyes met, and I mumbled, "So, this is where you live. It's so cozy … and you cook. Not many men in this country could be bothered."

"I learned in the army. It's fun to experiment in the kitchen. I use my imagination. And what about you? Do you like to cook?"

"I can only make pies. But it bores me. I don't like

standing by the stove. It's humiliating and oppressing for women. Were you a soldier?"

"Yes. Otherwise, I wouldn't have been able to travel out of the country."

"How did you look in uniform? Do you have a picture?"

"It's hanging in my mother's bedroom."

"Can't she send it to you?"

"I don't think so. But I would like to show you both that and some other pictures." Pablo took a deep breath and continued. "There's something I have to tell you. I think we belong together. That might sound weird. I had an inexplicable urge to come to your country. And now I know you are the one I've been waiting for. Fate wanted us to meet. My contract with the factory expires in a few months. I want you to come to Chile with me."

"Fate. I thought you said you weren't religious?"

"Fate has nothing to do with religion. It's something we're born with."

"How can poor people change their lives if they are born with a certain fate?"

"You *can* change your fate. You can work to change an unjust society. We attract or repel certain people. It's not by chance that we meet the people with whom we are to carry out duties."

"Duties?"

"Missions. So that future generations can benefit from our work and our choices."

"What's your mission?"

"To help build Chile as a country where women and men are equal, where there is no hunger, where every child can go to school, where there is a home for everyone, and where workers have the same rights as the wealthy. A country where solidarity and community reign."

"That's what all the apparatchiks in this country say too. I don't know whether it's really the workers who decide on self-government in Yugoslavia. It's as if they are sometimes used as a means to gain more power. It's difficult to see what's going on. Then again, we are sure we will get free medical help, education, a pension, and money to support ourselves. And we can travel to other countries."

"I like talking to you. I feel good in your company."

Pablo poured red wine into two transparent, polished crystal glasses and handed one to me. We toasted. The clinking sound cut through the stillness of the evening. The North Star illuminated the space between the cypresses in the garden as I sipped the wine. Pablo sent me a smile that overpowered me and made my heart beat wildly as he asked, "Are you sure you want to marry that man?"

"It's why I came to Dubrovnik."

"It looks that way on the surface, but actually you're here to meet me. That is the deeper meaning. He is not the man for you."

"How do you know when you've met the one?"

"You know when you listen to your inner self. It's a question of practice."

"Mmm, I don't know … I like you, but my life is quite complicated. And we haven't even slept with each other yet. I need more time to figure this out. It's all so overwhelming."

Pablo looked deep into my eyes as he said, "If you need more time, then take more time. But know that you live in my heart."

He got up and went to the open window. As if drawn, I followed him and put my hand in his.

It was a dark, moonless night. The stars fought over being the first to wave down to us. An oval spot didn't want to show its light but tried to hide behind a white veil. It was the Andromeda Galaxy. I was lucky. My grandmother had said it was usually difficult to spot. With its 300 billion stars, it was more than 2 million light years from our planet. Until about a hundred years ago, it was believed the Milky Way was the entire universe, and now here I was looking at Andromeda. Pablo's life and mine seemed like a drop, an atom, compared to the distant, shy organisms sending their energies down to us, to our minds. Were those creatures using their ethereal influence to control my life by dumping the man I was now embracing into it?

***

Summer at last. I graduated from business school. Done with toiling in school and listening to the teachers' tiring lectures. Done with reading into the early hours. Reaching a goal felt good, but I doubted whether a business degree was right for me. Either way, I had no desire to stand in some store selling bags or clothes or sit in an office serving male bosses. And an acting career wasn't just around the corner, even though I was good at acting and singing in the school theater. As student council rep and a scout, I knew how to organize and delegate work and tasks. I discussed social issues and politics, something I had learned at home. And I had experience from my time as a member of the local youth club. Maybe I could be the leader of a political organization? Several organizations needed revitalizing. One reform could be banning the use of political phrases and clichés, another could be introducing a critical review of the management structure—I just didn't know what Niko would say to my ambitions. We hadn't talked about what I wanted to do after business school.

***

Niko operated on everything from appendicitis to gallstones. The management at the hospital was satisfied with his work and promised him an apartment, maybe as early as in six months. "That suits our plans nicely," he said. He too was tired of living in a rented room and sharing the kitchen and bathroom with a stranger.

He invited me out to dinner to celebrate the good news. He looked tired; his work demanded great concentration. But he was happy. "It was good that you came to Dubrovnik with me, my love. I don't know what I'd have done without you. Living in a completely different city and establishing a new life, career, friends, getting used to the climate—none of that is easy." Niko's face grew serious. There was something he wanted to confide in me.

"I know you liked my military service and my soldier's uniform. But I actually couldn't bear being a soldier. Having to obey orders was vile. And I was afraid war would break out, and I would be sent to the front. No, I'm more into Brahms and Nat King Cole than weapons." He took a deep breath. "I think you should throw away my soldier's button."

Niko called every day and asked if we could see each other. I made excuses, mostly that I had to help Lina with her school work. Instead I was with Pablo.

It was as if Niko sensed something was wrong. One evening he called and threatened, "It's now or never. You need to set a date. That is why you're here, isn't it?"

"I'll set a date …" I said.

But before I could continue, he interrupted, "Call tomorrow and tell me when. The wedding has to happen within the month.

"Why the rush? I'm not pregnant."

"I have waited long enough. I want to move on with my life. Do you want me or not? You have to choose. Now!"

***

I stood in front of the mirror in the bathroom in Emma's apartment, applying mascara. It was a bright and humid June evening. Sweat trickled down my body even though I had only just rinsed myself with cold water. A large fly buzzed over my head, past a spider above the mirror, and landed on a bottle of perfume. The spider began to circle its web, jerking the threads. It rose on its legs, turned, and looked at me with all its teeny tiny eyes. It stared and stared, and suddenly the web gave way and collapsed. The spider plummeted and landed on my big toe. Terrified at the sight of its spindly legs, I raced out of the bathroom.

Lina was waiting in the living room and asked what had happened.

"I just got my period. It's early and I have no sanitary pads. Do you have any?"

She went into the bathroom, found some pads for me, and told me she had gotten her period too.

Lina and I went out. The evening breeze greeted us, and we walked down the steep steps to the stone-paved pedestrian street, Stradun, where we turned down an alley. Illuminated by the dim light of the streetlamps from the previous century, clotheslines hung heavily with white sheets and ladies' white underwear outside the shuttered windows. It was twilight. I looked up at the sky, it was blue with stars. A shooting star fell and Andromeda's left foot glistened as it pushed its halo. My stomach flipped. I spent too much time looking at the stars, my father said, I should stay more down to earth. But he didn't know you could ignite star-threads that invisibly bound people and stars to each other. Grandma knew it. On hot summer vacation evenings, she told us about the secret lives of the stars while the vines slept in the Herzegovinian village. She had been brought here from distant Odessa to experience love, despite her family being against it and abandoning her after she left the Hasidic community. But she had the stars. "They don't know about boundaries and religions," she said. "Only eternity."

The fragrance of oleanders drew me back to the sun-warmed stones of the street. Far away in an alley, love-sick guitar strings could be heard. A little farther away, a piercing rock and roll bass guitar and drums. Lina and I were approaching the disco.

We drank rum and Coke in the bar, a spotlight flashed. Lina chatted with an actor who I had seen in several feature films and TV series. Spotting someone she knew, she hurried over to her, leaving me with the actor. I didn't know what to do, so I said, "You look sad. In movies, you bring down women with a smile."

"Films are fantasy and role-playing, and I'm good at borrowing people's souls, but actually I'm shy and clumsy. I'm Vinko by the way."

He said he had lost his girlfriend of four years. "We planned on getting married, but she said yes to someone else. Her parents didn't want her to have children with an atheist like me. Mad to think religion still has such influence. I thought it died with World War II. For religious fanatics, what you are like as a person is less important. It's long-standing traditions that count. And money, even if the politicians preach equality and brotherhood. How could she agree to that? You women are world champions in playing double roles. You think only about having a safety net."

Vinko shed a tear. I don't know why, but I told him I didn't know if I was ready for the "one," and he said, "I think we need a drink. How about another rum and Coke?"

I must have gotten drunk. Suddenly I found myself in Vinko's apartment. We lay down. His sheets smelled of lavender, and he told me how the cleaning lady put little bags of lavender under the pillows.

I thought of a movie where he'd played a passionate lover on a beach. Loads of girls would have given anything in the world just to be allowed to touch his shirt. And here I was lying with him, being waited on by the charmer himself.

When I got up to leave, he asked if we could see each other the next day. I said yes, even though I was meeting Niko.

A bouquet of lilies was placed in the center of a round table set with large, flowered plates, tall wine glasses, and red napkins. We were going to eat the chicken dish Vinko had eaten every day for two weeks when in Paris the previous year, and we were to drink homemade wine that smelled of fig and carob. The antique cherry table we were eating at went wherever he traveled with his film crew. It was even going to follow him when, shortly, he would head to the mountains north of the city where a new film, a West German western, was to be shot. It was his first role in a foreign film. He explained it was important to him even though he only had a supporting role. It could lead to more film roles abroad. "But why take a table everywhere?" I asked.

"It's lucky," he replied convincingly, not caring

whether people on the film crew thought he had a screw loose.

He shared what it was like to go skiing with other actors, what the most expensive caviar in the world tasted like, and how he'd learned little tricks to conquer a woman.

I spent the next day with Vinko again. We ate the same French chicken dish and drank the wine that smelled of fig and carob. And went to the disco. He wanted to listen to loud music. "Fine with me," I said.

They played Cliff Richard and The Young Ones that night. We danced the last dance. Vinko started to kiss my neck, my naked shoulders. My body quivered. He took me in his arms and pulled me to him. Our bodies were glued together. Looking deep into my eyes, he said it was good I had come. He had been afraid I wouldn't see him again.

Without hesitation, I said, "I've canceled my wedding to Niko. And I broke up with the Chilean. His fantasies were getting on my nerves. I'd rather be with you."

Vinko gave me a long kiss. I licked his lips with my tongue. We became more and more impassioned, sinking into a trance-like state of long kisses and lack of air …

A man dancing next to us poked me in the back. I removed the hair from my face and turned around.

There stood Pablo, staring with his green eyes. He said, "I had serious plans for you, but you are not at all mature. You don't care who you get together with."

Pablo disappeared, and I remained standing on the dance floor without moving, without blinking. It was as if he had awakened a longing in me that had thus far lain dormant.

I was seized with panic, started scolding Vinko, and ran away, sobbing.

***

"You can't live on oranges!" screamed Emma.

I had to eat proper food, or I would get sick, and she wouldn't be able to look my mother in the eye if something happened to me.

She made suggestions about what I could do instead of lying in bed staring at the sky. Go out and have fun, watch a movie, go to a café, read a good book. I could borrow one of her biology books and read about how plants convert carbon dioxide into the oxygen we breathe. "We should be grateful we are alive," she said. "You'll meet a man who will make you happy."

I no longer listened to Emma but fantasized about embracing Pablo's body, smelling his skin, holding his hand, playing with his fingers, kissing him … I had to speak to him. Tell him I couldn't live without him, he had enchanted me, I had never had this feeling before.

When I told Emma I was planning on visiting Pablo, she wanted to come with me. "You never know what ideas he might get. And what would your father say? He's not exactly in favor of you marrying a foreigner unless he's an American. Pablo may only be pretending to be *the sweet Pablo* but in reality is a different person entirely. Tito has invited many peculiar foreigners to our country. They have a different culture. What's worse, they can be quite insistent toward our girls. They probably don't get anything from their own women before they're married. We can't invite all kinds of students and engineers just because their countries are in Tito's Non-Alignment Movement. They don't even stay here when they finish their education. And yet, still, they get almost everything handed to them."

"But Pablo is here to build Yugoslavia," I said, annoyed.

Emma fell silent, and we took the tram to the south of the city.

People smiled as if they were mocking me.

The evening scent of oleander and jasmine had settled heavily in Pablo's atrium garden when we got to his house. There was light in the living room. Emma and I climbed onto a garden table and spotted Pablo.

He was sitting on the sofa, staring into space.

"Ring the bell," Emma mumbled.

I jumped down, straightened my clothes, and rang the bell. Pablo opened the door cautiously. When he realized who was standing there, he threw himself into my arms and held me tight.

The cicadas sang in the shade of the olive leaves. The swallows circled overhead, chirping. The smell of incense from the nearby church touched my nose. Pablo asked in a deep, full voice, "Will you marry me?"

I made no reply, only nodded and surrendered to his irresistible power, which was perhaps fate.

Andromeda's eye winked at the gas and dust of the Milky Way where stars were born.

***

The amethyst-blue sky leaned against the medieval

walls surrounding the old part of Dubrovnik. The walls stood proud, watching the high waves that crashed against their feet. The waves rushed across small pebble beaches and back to the sea where they came from.

Party-clad people speaking all kinds of languages gathered in the city's squares and churches to hear Renaissance music. The summer festival had begun.

Pablo and I held hands as we ran out of the city hall. Emma and Lina followed quickly behind, throwing rice and olive twigs at us. I looked up at Pablo admiringly and heard him say, "I love you, Mrs. Morena. If only my mother could see you. I'm sure she would like you."

I started laughing. "Are all Chilean men as happy with their mother as you are?"

"I'm not just happy with my mother, I love her very much. And she is faithful. I hope you will be just as faithful, my love."

5

THE FORTUNE TELLER
SARAJEVO, 1965

The whole family now knew I was in happy circumstances. It had happened *after* Pablo and I were married, my mother pointed out when she visited her siblings and friends.

My mother was already sewing a maternity dress inspired by the movie *Cleopatra* with Elizabeth Taylor. A white dress without a belt and a dark tunic with white stars.

We had moved in with my parents and were waiting for Pablo to get his old job back so we could move to Santiago.

My brother, Robert, couldn't stand sleeping in the living room, so he spent most of the time with his fiancée, who lived nearby. Her name was Kana, and she came from Srebrenica, a town in Eastern Bosnia known for its spa.

Everything had become more expensive, but my father's wages had not increased correspondingly. Pablo treated his in-laws to a trip to the spa, and when they returned to Sarajevo after a few weeks' stay, they were rested and refreshed. Pablo also paid the rent and the household expenses, so now you could no longer hear my mother and father quarreling. Niko was right when he'd once said his parents fell out because of lack of money.

My father's anger that I married a foreigner had vanished. Now he had someone with whom he could play chess and discuss politics. "Tito is the only one who can bring together the alignment movement-free countries across culture and religion. It all comes down to creating lasting peace and letting the workers decide on the means of production. In this country, we call it self-government. But the rich countries continue their colonialization, just in a more sophisticated way. They allow themselves to be represented by the insiders they bribe. As long as that continues, there will be no peace."

Pablo nodded affirmatively, adding, "Our movement in Chile will introduce a political and economic system that resembles yours. We are fighting for workers' rights, but I am afraid that the capitalist world is advancing faster and will decide the rules of the game. Capitalism is changing people's way of thinking, pacifying us with television, advertising, and sex."

My father's eyes sparkled. "I must admit I'm a little

fascinated by the American system, even though it rests on capitalism. You have the opportunity to use your skills and achieve what you want. You are the creator of your own luck. If only you could combine their political system and ours. But it's as if people can't figure out how to find a golden mean. It's either or."

He rolled his eyes and stood up. Took a carafe of schnapps and two small glasses from the display cabinet. My mother served nibbles of cheese, tomatoes, and sausage.

***

After lunch, Robert's fiancée, Kana, suggested the two of us go for a walk and let Pablo and Robert talk about "men's affairs." It was a cool autumn day. The clouds sailed away, driven by the furious wind.

We walked toward the chestnut avenue on the other side of the bridge. Kana told me she and Robert would like to live together, but they couldn't afford to rent an apartment yet. She had just started work as an elementary school teacher, which she was happy about. But she was not much in favor of teaching Cyrillic letters. "The vast majority of the people of our republic don't use those letters. It's enough that our pupils learn the Latin alphabet. And now the oldest students are to be taught military skills and defense ..."

I interrupted her. "Isn't it good that the pupils learn Cyrillic too? Then it's easier for them to learn Russian, which is the main language along with English. And military skills are necessary in our time. We can't count on anyone coming to our rescue if the country is attacked. We will have to defend ourselves—"

I was about to go on, but suddenly my wedding ring slipped off my finger and onto the pavement. When I bent down to pick up the ring and put it on, Kana yelled, "That's not a good sign. It's an omen of divorce!"

What is she going on about? I thought and said angrily, "You say you're not religious, but you're certainly superstitious. It's not exactly the right image for a teacher."

Kana fell silent. Her face stiffened. The rain began to drip. The wind whipped through my windbreaker. I put my hands in my pockets to warm them. In the left pocket, I felt something round and took it out to see what it was.

Niko's soldier's button with its red star in the middle lay shining in my hand. My stomach lurched. I closed my hand quickly and put the button back in my pocket. Kana asked what it was. I said it was a button I had forgotten to sew onto my windbreaker, that was why I was freezing.

Something stirred in the underbrush near us. The dark chestnut leaves rustled.

***

Six-week-old Alberto was swaddled in warm clothes and blankets so the cold wouldn't seep through the pram, which got covered in snow as soon as it was put outside. No one could remember the last time it had snowed this much in April.

I pushed the pram faster and faster and suddenly there was the house. The house where Flora was visiting someone she knew. I wanted to say farewell before I left for Chile. Flora opened the door and said in surprise, "How did you know I was here?"

"Your mother told me. But she didn't know when you'd be home. We leave for Santiago early tomorrow morning. I just want to say goodbye. Am I disturbing you?"

"Not at all. I'm visiting one of Tilda's old acquaintances. Come in. And you have little Alberto with you! Can I hold him?"

"Of course."

Flora walked in with Alberto in her arms. I followed.

An old woman with long white hair and blurry eyes sat on the couch in the living room, massaging her right leg as she rocked back and forth. She spoke an ancient language, as if she belonged to some primeval time and had come from another planet. Flora hadn't told me about her. Why was she at her house? Perhaps because she missed her grandmother, Tilda.

The old woman insisted on telling me my future with white beans. Maybe it was the same fortune teller who got Niko's sperm back when I thought I was to be his. I don't know why I agreed to having my fortune told. I didn't really feel like it.

The woman retrieved a round wooden bowl from a drawer, uncovered it, grabbed a handful of white beans, placed them carefully on the table, and counted them. They were all there. Forty-one in total. Then she grabbed the beans with her right hand, which she covered with her left, and raised her hands to her mouth, whispering. When she was done with the incantation, she put the beans back on the table, divided them into three groups, and then into smaller groups again that became patterns. She scrutinized the patterns and repeated the ritual twice. Other patterns appeared. When she finished interpreting, she said with seriousness in her voice, "It would have been better if you had waited to have children. When children are born early in marriage, it will not be a happy one."

I got up, put on my coat, said a quick goodbye, grabbed the pram with the sleeping Alberto, and hurried away from the house.

It started to snow. A crushing heaviness crept into my chest.

6

ROSALIA AND RAFAEL
SANTIAGO, 1966–1969

Kana, now my sister-in-law after having married Robert, called regularly to ask how Pablo and I were doing. She pretended to be concerned and wanted to know if we were still together. At first, I didn't understand her hints, but one day it dawned on me she still thought we were going to divorce because of the time my wedding ring slipped off my finger.

Annoyed, I replied, "Don't you have anything better to think about? How about your own marriage. Robert is close to breaking due to your eternal complaining. I have had enough. I will not put up with your insinuations anymore!"

My voice went to such a high frequency that she hung up.

I was relieved. That's how it feels to be strong, I thought. For the first time I realized how much power was hidden in words. How much you could accomplish with the right turn of phrase at the right time and be satisfied with yourself.

On the streets of Santiago, everyone smiled and gave each other kisses.

***

Pablo's mother and father lived on the same street as us. One day Pablo suggested that Rosalia, his mother, look after Alberto. Something in me protested, so I said, "But I'll be at home, that's not necessary. Your mother can watch him when we go out."

"But then you won't have any time for yourself, my love. She can help you with the day-to-day chores. You can ask her about anything if you have any doubts."

"Thank you, but I prefer to look after Alberto myself. She is welcome to help with the food every so often when I need it."

"Are you saying you are going to take care of Alberto on your own? He is not to be taken care of. He needs to be raised! We must make him a proper citizen of this society. And my mother can easily do that."

"But I'm still breastfeeding him. It's far too early to think of him as a citizen. He has plenty of time."

"You are breastfeeding, but I'm not sure you should continue to do so for too much longer. The health authorities recommend bottled milk or powdered milk.

Many mothers stop breastfeeding. It's not good for the breasts either. You'll end up looking like … I don't know what if you breastfeed all our future children."

"The authorities need women in the workforce. They don't dare say it outright. That's why we now have to give children bottles. But the fact is that mother's milk is the best food for babies. Nothing else can replace it. I will not harm my child."

***

When we got home after seeing *Swan Lake* with the Russian prima ballerina Maya Plisetskaya, Alberto was full of energy, crawling from one side of the living room to the other. With Rosalia! The girl who had been looking after him wasn't there, even though that was who had said goodbye to us when we went out. What was Rosalia doing there? I thought.

She said she had wanted to spend the evening with her grandson, so she had sent the girl home. Rosalia could see I was boiling over with rage and excitedly exclaimed, "Now let me show you what your clever son can do."

She turned to Alberto and said smiling, "Alberto, say what Grandma taught you. Come on, darling."

Alberto glanced hesitantly at Rosalia and looked like he was about to cry. But then he opened his mouth and mumbled something that sounded like, "... *mi abuela*"—my grandma.

Rosalia clapped.

***

Pablo's father, Rafael, was a cardiologist at the hospital in Santiago. He worked ten hours at a time and had rotating shifts, so he rarely visited us. But when he opened the hall door, he used to conjure something out of his jacket for me—books, women's magazines, or ornamented faience bowls.

One day he invited me to a café. He was curious to know how I was doing in my new country. I wanted to say his wife's meddling got on my nerves, his son was too attached to his mother and insistent on following her advice on how to raise children, I felt lonely, and that my only friends were also Pablo's friends, specifically Jorge and his wife, Maria. Instead I said things were going well, and I was still having a little trouble with my Spanish. I mixed up the tenses and lacked the words to express myself properly.

He didn't think I needed to worry about it. "You speak Spanish well. You get better and better every time we meet. Don't worry about that. But it must be hard—living in a new country, new surroundings, different people. Just know, if my wife meddles too much in your lives, you must tell me, and I will talk to her. And I realize Pablo believes his mother knows best, but don't give in so easily. He is still stubborn, but you must insist on talking to him if you have a problem. He can have good ideas. Try to convince him that other truths exist, but do it gently. Don't get angry with him. It will do you no good. The only person who will suffer is you. Don't dwell too much on the negative and forget to look ahead. Get out and have fun! Perhaps dancing is something for you?"

Rafael introduced me to his favorite writers, Borges and Marques. Their books made him a better person, a better husband even, he said. In the books, he even found "recipes" on how to better understand women, including his own wife.

Rosalia turned up at our home from time to time. Prying, examining everything, and becoming a fixture. She cooked lentil soup and meat in pastry, brought cuttings for the window box, toys for Alberto, and was even already buying clothes for our future child. But when she brought a crystal vase, Pablo exclaimed, "That's enough! Thanks for your gifts, but Masha has everything she needs. You should give the gifts to the poor instead. And Mother, Masha would like to talk to you about baby formula, wouldn't you, my love?"

Rosalia smiled as though content with life.

***

I called Flora once a month, but one evening she called me. It was almost midnight, and I was restless. Something happened, I thought.

But she just said she was getting married. She and her husband-to-be had only been together for two months, but she knew it was serious. "I'm pregnant. Unfortunately my mother did not get to hear my news. She died five days ago. She was only forty-nine."

Choking back tears, Flora went on. "I do not know what's happening. It's as if someone has cursed me and my family. I made sure not to get pregnant, and he did too. Still, it happened … and my mother is no longer here. I don't know how I'm going to get through my final piano recital at the music conservatory."

Seven months later, Flora called to say the piano recital had gone well, and she had given birth to a son. Jasha was his name. That same day I gave birth to a daughter, our second child. We named her Alma.

Flora did not call again. I called a few times, but later I stopped contacting her completely.

Kana didn't call anymore either. I didn't care if they called or if I had to call them. I no longer thought about what they were doing and how they were feeling. Their lives took on less and less significance in terms of my existence.

At night I was awakened by Alma's crying. Or else I lay in bed thinking about something I was worried about. Was I in a state to handle marriage? The children? Was this really the life I wanted? What had become of my dreams and ambitions? What was I doing in a foreign country among strangers? It was difficult to understand their temperament, their way of doing things, their culture. And Pablo. He had changed. I no longer knew whether he genuinely loved me. Sometimes he seemed distant, unreachable, cynical. When he made love to me, I was his *querida*, his love. When he was annoyed with me, he yelled *caramba*, damn! Or had *I* changed so much I couldn't recognize myself anymore? I began to doubt my love for him. I grew more and more annoyed.

7
You Don't Say No to the President
Santiago, 1970

The bedside lamp in the bedroom was turned off as I lay in bed dozing with my eyes open. I tried to get up, but I couldn't see the lamp because of my stomach. I was expecting our third child. Alma was crying next door. I felt life slipping away from me. The air was wet with the heavy rain of twilight. You could hear the raindrops bursting out on the terrace. At the same moment, the door opened. Breathless, Pablo said, "Salvador has won! He wants me to be his right hand, *querida*. We are free! The manor estates are to be parceled out and all copper mines nationalized! People will get higher wages, affordable apartments, free health care ..."

Pablo worked from seven in the morning until six in the evening, but on Sundays, he took Alberto by the hand, I put Alma in the pram, and we strolled over to Jorge and Maria's. The men sat in the living room playing chess, drinking, and eating spicy *longaniza* sausage. Jorge's wife and I sat in the kitchen drinking tea and discussing women's oppression while Alberto and their daughter, Isabella, sat at the dining room table playing dominoes. When the men had finished playing chess, they threw themselves into political debates. Pablo talked about Salvador, about how he'd found evidence foreign companies had earned fortunes from Chilean copper and evaded the tax. "Now they can't cheat us anymore. The oppression of workers is over. We hold the power in our hands."

Jorge added, "We have to revise history."

It was after one of our many visits to Jorge and Maria's that Pablo, with a serious and ominous expression on his face, told us we had to move. I asked innocently, "Who's moving?"

"You, me, and the children." His voice sounded menacing. "We have to start packing tonight. We're moving tomorrow".

I was scared. "Why won't you tell me more? What's going on?"

"Salvador has given me an important job. I am to be general manager of the world's largest copper mine."

It was the Chuquicamata mine in the Atacama Desert. The mine was nationalized under Allende. Pablo had once told me that Che Guevara had stayed at the mine in 1952 during his motorcycle tour of South

America, and Fidel Castro had given a speech to the miners about the situation in the world and the fiercely fluctuating prices of copper. But I couldn't get my head around Pablo wanting the whole family to live in a place like that. I shouted, "That's a long, long way from Santiago. Why didn't you ask *me* first?"

"How can you say such a thing? *Caramba!*" roared Pablo. "You don't say no to the president! And *I* wanted this. I have dreamed about the workers getting power over the mine for a long time."

Pablo paused, his voice becoming amorous. "You can also get a job, *querida*. The miners' wives have opened a school. You can be a teacher or work in the new library."

The next morning a truck stopped and picked up our belongings. We drove by car to the airport, and the plane flew north.

I forgot to say I would miss Santiago.

8
THE SOLDIER BUTTON
CHUQUICAMATA, 1970–1971

The door to a green colonial-style house with a white bay window in the middle and carved yellow balconies was open when we arrived at a small town about six miles from the copper mine. A dark plump woman with smiling eyes greeted us and welcomed us. Sarita was her name. She was to live in an annex behind the house and cook and watch the children when I wasn't home.

Out of breath after helping us bring the suitcases in, she took Alma on her lap and said, "This is a lively little girl you have. She's a bundle of energy. It's unlikely she'll end up here in the desert's ghostly landscape. I sense her soul far away from this place."

Sarita fell into a reverie, and as if she were suddenly waking up, in a melancholic, singsong voice, she said, "I have missed children. My husband and I didn't manage to have any. He was killed in a mining accident. It happened the day after he found an old mummy in the sand at the mine. He looked startled when he came

70

home that day. He wouldn't talk to me; just said he saw a man with shining eyes and a wide-open mouth."

Sarita lifted her head and looked at me. "Mrs. Morena, I see that you will give birth soon. It will be a boy. I can help you with the birth."

The house had a patio in the middle, three large rooms, and two small ones with writing bureaus, chests of drawers, beds, and mirrors. Sarita had made dinner, brown beans in coriander sauce.

That evening, after Pablo and I had said good night to Alberto and Alma, we went out on the terrace. It was as if the sky, filled with leaping crystal-twinkling stars, were about to tumble into the house. The closest stars kissed the steppes while Andromeda shook with laughter from her fixed place on the northwest side. A large knight-like figure of copper blazed like fire as if it had borrowed the light of the stars to warm us in the chilly wind.

We rushed into the bedroom. Pablo put a Victor Jara record on the gramophone. He put his arms around my waist, took off my dress, my bra, my panties, and kissed me tenderly and intensely. I didn't think I could be turned on with a big belly, but Pablo's touches caused little detonations, my blood boiled, and the baby kicked as if he himself were there.

Pablo carried me and my belly to the bathroom, carefully laid me down in the tub, and turned on the faucets. He hastily removed his clothes, sat down next to me, and put a splash of rose oil in the water. We started touching each other, kissed, and let the warm water splash over our faces and bodies.

***

Sarita was right. I gave birth to a son. Augusto. But she wasn't the only one who helped me with the labor. Pablo had to call a doctor when the baby didn't want to come out. The doctor lived in the house next door, which lay next to an old white church that consisted essentially of only the church steeple. At seven in the morning, as the church bells rang, Augusto was born. The doctor had smeared my thighs and the area around the opening of my vagina with a salve of jasmine and nutmeg. He lit frankincense, incense extracted from the Boswellia tree, which for several thousand years was as valuable as gold. I let myself drift away.

I was woken by whinnying and blowing in front of the house. When I came out, Pablo was standing there with a big, dark-brown horse. It turned and looked at me. It stood still and beautiful, and I went to it immediately as if attracted by a magnet. Patted it on the side. Warm air streamed out of its muzzle.

The horse sniffed my right hand. I ran my hands over its back with my eyes closed. The luminous silhouette of a person appeared before me and told me silently that my old horse from my father's village had returned. It gave me a start, and I opened my eyes.

Astonished, Pablo said, "It's as if the horse knows you. I bought it from Sarita's brother. He needs the money to repair the family house. Now the horse is yours. His name is Helios. He can help you explore the area."

With me on his back, Helios rode to salt mountains and crater-like hollows. He was tethered to a small rock that looked like an eagle. I sat down on the sandy reddish earth and waited for sunset.

Once, Helios took me to a hot spring. It was hidden behind a rock that resembled a dragon. I took off my clothes, plunged into the warm water, inhaled the sulfurous smell, submerged myself to my collarbone, and stayed in the water and steam until I began to lick the sweat from my lips. When I put my clothes on, Helios was ready to leave.

A cool sea current from the Pacific brought us to an Incan fort. Sarita had spoken of "mysterious events" she'd experienced there. I tried to get Helios to stop, but he bristled and started to rear and neigh as if sensing something scary and galloped away from the spot without my permission.

Far out on the horizon, a white volcanic peak that looked like a woman's breast could be seen. It made me rush home to nurse Augusto and help Alberto with his math.

When Helios and I approached the mine area, smoke was still pouring out of the mine's chimney. Somewhere in the office building Pablo was sitting at his desk or inspecting the production in the factory and talking to the workers. But every time I saw the mine, I felt sad, without knowing why. Helios trampled the earth and galloped away.

***

Alberto kept asking for his father when he came home from school. He wanted to play with Pablo, he said. I had to calm him down, called him Comrade Alberto. The word *comrade* evoked a proud expression on his face, and he forgot his father was not home.

Augusto had finally fallen asleep after Sarita gave him fennel tea for a stomachache. I watched over his crib in the bedroom, but just as I was about to go to sleep, I spotted a piece of paper on the double bed with the words: *I miss you.*

I heard Pablo open the front door and his steps on the stairs. He rushed into the bedroom. I said I had missed him too. So did Alberto. We didn't see that much of him, I said and asked if he could take a day off once in a while. Pablo's eyebrows shot up as he said, "I want to be in solidarity with and contribute to the community. But as soon as I finish my job, we can go back to Santiago."

I said no more but grew sorrowful at the thought of leaving Sarita, Helios, and the desert. Here I was free from Rosalia's advice about how I should talk to the children, what they should eat, read, and who they should spend time with.

I took my bathrobe off and put it on the chair in front of the dressing table but heard something fall out of the pocket. I bent down to see what it was. Niko's soldier button shone in the moonlight. I picked it up, caressed it, put it in the pocket of my favorite dress, and decided the button was to come everywhere and get to know all my pockets.

***

I woke to the sound of someone descending the stairs. Then a creak and something fell. I ran down and opened the hall door. Alberto's shadow disappeared into the darkness. My hands shook.

When I asked the next morning where he had been, he looked at me strangely and said he had been asleep, of course.

Alberto's nightly wanderings continued. One night I sat awake in bed waiting for his steps. It was two o'clock in the morning when I heard him coming down the stairs. Quietly I went out into the hall and saw him open the window. He climbed up onto the windowsill and jumped down. I opened the hall door and went after him. When I caught up with him, his blurry eyes were shining. His gaze was blank and stiff. I opened my mouth to say something, but no sound came from my throat.

Alberto trudged around the house, the pepper trees, around holes and bumps. I followed. At once he turned and strode toward the house. The window was still open. Alberto crawled up, jumped down, and disappeared back into his room.

I remained standing on the gravel path in front of the house.

The stars in the sky rocked and pushed the great moon, which hung like a majestic white ball, untouchable with its birthmarks while yet another child's soul was caught in its web.

***

The new library was located in the only square in town. It was an old house that had been restored by the residents. Children and adults sat on benches, leafing through books.

At the school, which was in an azure-blue oblong building beside it, the teachers taught Alberto and the other pupils about equality and freedom.

Were the two concepts important for Alberto to learn? Had his little brain become confused by school and was that perhaps why he had contracted moonsickness? Did I myself truly know what the terms entailed? Freedom—everyone knew what that was, but equality—that was more difficult to understand. It must mean striving for everyone to have the opportunity to get an education and a job, regardless of who they were and where they came from. But people could never be completely equal. There were those who were very clever, those less clever, those who were stupid, those with mental health issues and physical disabilities, those who were better at dealing with life because they were intelligent and more creative than others, and those whose parents were better off or had a higher education. Regardless, if you created good opportunities for everyone, then more people would get chances, and then they could be better at helping each other.

***

I missed working in a professional community.

After much consideration, Pablo agreed to hire a girl to watch the children, so I could work in the library where they needed a library assistant.

There weren't that many books to shelve in the library. Still, there was something for everyone—literary classics, mostly Russian, books about healing herbs, children's books from distant lands, and books on weapons and civil defense.

The library bookkeeper sat in a corner with his head bent over stacks of papers. And then there was a librarian who was responsible for which books we were permitted to buy and what the children were allowed to read. She could quote from Karl Marx's *Das Kapital*, especially about the "Utilization of the elements of the labor force," and from Vladimir Ilyich Lenin's *April Theses*. She wore dresses with at least two pockets that were stuffed with remnants of fabric. She used them to blow her nose. She often had a cold, and teachers, pupils, housewives with small children, miners, everyone who visited the library, asked about her health. She thanked them and said she was feeling better and recommended a book they should absolutely read.

Afterward, all the library's visitors sat reading without moving.

***

Pablo didn't talk about his work and made no reply

whenever I asked. I began to wonder what he was actually doing. I imagined him surrounded by the women who worked in the mine. They waited on him with food and drink and perhaps offered their bodies. Several of them had neither a husband nor a boyfriend.

But the moment Pablo came through the door after work, I forgot all about the potential competitors. He kissed me like he genuinely missed me.

He missed his mother too and suggested we invite her to stay with us for a while. "She hasn't even seen Augusto. She could help look after the children."

I told him I was quite happy with the nanny, but Pablo said, "The nanny can't even read to the children or tell them how to sit at the table."

"You play at being a worker, but when it comes down to it you are middle class. You can't let go of what you were brought up with. You *are* and will *always* be your mother's boy."

"Do you realize how important I am to the workers? This society cannot exist without me. And never speak badly about my mother. Is that understood?"

Pablo's blue-green eyes flashed with anger.

At long last a letter from Robert! He had long since graduated as an engineer. Kana was still working as a teacher. But they were fighting a lot. Maybe because they didn't have any children. Maybe because he was jealous, he wrote. She was older than him but still looked like a young girl.

The other day, when they'd had guests, he was the one who had started quarreling, he admitted. He accused her of looking at their male guest in a certain way that caused the guest to follow her into the kitchen. But Kana said he was imagining things and began to scold him. "You could hear her shouts up and down the entire stairwell of the apartment block," he wrote. He signed off the letter with the conclusion, "We're not compatible anymore."

9
Anna
Santiago 1973

September 11. General Augusto Pinochet's junta bombs the presidential palace. Congress is dissolved. Popular Unity, led by President Salvador Allende, is crushed.

Pinochet announces on the radio that the president has committed suicide.

***

We had moved back to Santiago and were living in an apartment in the city center. I was six months pregnant—we were expecting our fourth child. Pablo was working in the presidential palace. But that morning he was at home. We knew Salvador had not taken his own life. "He was murdered," said Pablo. His voice shook.

"The same people were behind the demonstrations three years ago when he was inaugurated as president. Do you remember the youths who marched in the streets of Santiago? They swung chains and hit out with sticks. But Salvador refused to believe they were dangerous."

Several places in the city were cordoned off. Pablo called Jorge. When he hung up, he said he had to go. "I want to find out what is going on and what we have to do. I'll be back soon."

He went into the bedroom and kissed the sleeping children. "Say hi to them from me and tell them I love them."

He hurried off. His kiss turned into a quick peck. He couldn't hide the grief in his eyes.

Pablo didn't come home that night, but he called. It was safer for him to stay at Jorge's for a few days, he said, and he suggested I seek help at the Yugoslav embassy.

I called the next morning, but a voice said the ambassador wasn't accepting visitors.

The next day, a sunny morning, a military Jeep pulled up in front of the house. Four soldiers quickly got out, marched into the stairwell, and knocked on the door. I opened the door. Without saying anything, they grabbed my arm, pulled it, and shouted, "Get the children!"

"They're eating breakfast."

"Then tell them to stop!"

"They need to put clothes on."

"You have three minutes."

I hesitated.

"Do it, pig!" roared the youngest soldier.

Augusto burst into tears. Frantic, I began dressing the children. Alma screamed as we were pushed into the car.

After a few miles of driving, I realized we were on our way to the airport. The car stopped abruptly at departures. We were dragged out of the Jeep. A throng of photographers and journalists asked a lot of questions. I opened my mouth, but one of the soldiers pushed me forward.

A black Mercedes was parked a few yards away. The driver opened the door and started the engine. Two soldiers tore Augusto out of my arms and pushed me aside. Alma, who was almost five, was held down against the asphalt. Alberto, now eight, reached for her arm, but a soldier kicked him and threw him to the ground. Two-year-old Augusto stared at me, terrified. Two more soldiers hauled the children into the Mercedes and accelerated away. I tried to chase after the car, but it quickly vanished. My head was spinning ... I let myself collapse onto the tarmac.

I woke up feeling the cold. Then burgundy-colored tiles under me. Turned my head. I wasn't alone. Glimpsed two long legs in a military uniform. The boots encasing the legs were black. The trampling of boots told me I needed to get up. The stamping echoed piercingly sharp. Little by little I managed to come up to standing. My legs were tired and heavy. A long, narrow corridor with closed doors warned of intransigence.

To my right, the door was ajar. A beam of light revealed a dark-red stain on the tiles. On the door hung a sign with four words. It only said one thing: The Ministry of Defense. The soldier spoke loudly and emphasized each word. I was not to bow. I was not to squat. I was not to lie on the floor either, he added. Only stand. And wait. Wait to be brought into the General Staff Office where General Pinochet himself was, the soldier stressed.

In the room with the door ajar sat an officer with a serious face, leafing through some papers. He picked up the phone and turned the dial. I heard him say,

"The Yugoslav Embassy." His voice suddenly moved up a scale. "She is accused of putting 50,000 fake dollars into circulation. Will the embassy give her protection? … Did you say, *No, señor*?" asked the officer after which he slammed down the receiver.

The door to the room with the officer was closed. The beam of light disappeared. No voices. A dim lamp flickered as if the electrical bulb were emitting the last vital signs. I could no longer feel my legs. The numbness turned into pain. I thought about starting to count the minutes but refrained from doing so when the soldier who was keeping an eye on me stirred. I turned my head back a little and spotted a staircase. His face was expressionless. He had an elongated birthmark on one side of his face and neck as if a snake had crept up from the tightly buttoned uniform jacket. I cautiously asked if I could sit down. He looked at me with eyes swathed in hate. His whole head turned scarlet. His mouth quivered. The arteries in his neck stood out. The birthmark moved faster and faster. He shook me with his strong hands, and beads of sweat formed on his forehead. He pushed me toward the stairs, I grabbed his uniform, he kicked my hand with his boot, and I rolled down the stairs.

Blood ran out in circles around me and flowed down the steps. At the bottom step, I landed on my stomach. I felt a warm lump under the dress, but I couldn't touch or see the lost little person whose dreams would never come true. Darkness looked me in the eye.

My body floated in a mist. A vein was closing. But a mighty light pushed at the fog and shook my heart. Slowly my body tore itself free from the mist. A voice sounded as if through anesthesia. "She will die soon. Drive her to her father-in-law's house."

Rafael smiled when I woke up. Despite the curfew, he had crept out through the back of the house and fetched a doctor who had administered an injection against poisoning.

The next morning, at nine o'clock, there was a knock on the door. I was bleeding profusely. As soon as Rafael opened the door, two soldiers made their way into the hall. Rafael asked the soldiers to wait to get me, but one of them replied, "If you say more, we will kill you here, in your own house!"

A military vehicle was waiting outside the house. I was driven to the National Stadium.

An echo rattled around in my head: *Once you're brought to Estadio Nacional, you never come out alive again.*

***

The soldiers threw me into a cell. Women squatted. A thin young girl said, "Welcome to hell. You're number 66. Surprised? No, it's not a hotel. But you can sleep sitting up."

An elderly woman tugged the young girl's arm, and she fell silent.

A middle-aged woman with red eyes gave me her coat to sit on. Five or six others sat close to me. I warmed up. The old woman whispered, "You have to survive. Your children and your husband need you. One day you will get out and remember this place as a bad dream."

The thin girl took over. "When the executioners hurt you, don't think about the pain, use your inner voice to say, 'God bless you, executioner.' When you forgive, the pain disappears."

***

The hearings happened mostly at night. I was asked a barrage of questions: Why was Pablo a member of Allende's party? What was his job? Who were his friends? What were their names?

I was led to a room with a stone floor. The room rumbled with echoes. A blanket was put over my head, and I was ordered to stand. My swollen legs hurt. But the pain left when I heard gunshots in the room next door.

A woman screamed. She was being beaten. She screamed again. She was beaten. Her screams grew fainter. She fell. I was scared stiff.

Another woman was beaten. A shot rang out … I remembered no more.

When I awoke the blanket had been removed from my head. In one corner was a black table. On the table stood a tape recorder, two glasses, and two bottles of wine. Two men in civilian clothes ushered me out of the room. I looked around to get a glimpse of the other room I thought was next to. But there were no other rooms.

The next day the executioners came again. One of them said I was more dangerous than Pablo. "You filled his head with socialist ideas. You seduced him. First by fucking him and then by stuffing his head with your comrade Tito, comrade Lenin, and your comrade Marx. That's why you married him. Your job was to spread their sick ideologies by selling your body, you whore! You pig! You didn't deserve him! He doesn't love you anymore! He's found someone else. He said so himself. He's already forgotten all about you, you socialist bitch! You stink of working class!"

The soldier reeked of alcohol. His eyes shone with disgust. With a sleazy mouth, foaming at the corner, he screamed, "Now you get your just deserts!"

He stuck a long wire into a plug switch in the wall. Attached to the other end of the wire was something that resembled a pair of pliers … I fainted for a moment. It happened again.

More soldiers entered. They were six now. I was sitting on a high stool. My hands were tied with a chain. One of them asked questions. I stayed silent. Another one shouted. Another question. I didn't say anything. He screamed in my face. A third punched and kicked my legs, my kidneys, my back, my head. The fourth yanked my hair. The fifth slapped me. When the sixth spat on me, I roared, "Kill me! I hate you and your uniform! All uniforms, all soldiers! Kill me! I beg you!"

I woke up in the cell with bruises and wounds on my body.

The soldiers came to get me again. As they pushed me into an elliptical-shaped room one of them began to rip off my blouse. But another pushed him away and said in a loud voice, "Leave her alone! She's my cousin. What will I tell my aunt if she finds out? She'll kill me."

The soldier stopped peeling my clothes off, and they all started mocking the one who stopped me from being raped. He said he was going out to get something and I was to stay put. He went out and came back with a bowl in his hands. The steam from the hot tomato soup billowed up toward the damp ceiling. The soldier put the soup on a small table, handed me a cigarette, and lit it. I wanted to hug him as I let smoke pass my throat, fill my lungs, and numb my brain.

The next morning, they took me again. A soldier said they weren't going to interrogate me and added, "We just have to show you something."

I was pushed into a large room with white walls.

There was blood everywhere—on the floor, on the walls, on the ceiling. Another soldier pressed play on a tape recorder on a table in the middle of the room. The speakers crackled. There was a voice … Pablo's voice … it was interrupted by blows. Several blows. There was shouting and spitting. Pablo didn't answer the questions. A tormentor screamed. Someone kicked. A third one roared. Punches, kicks, shouts, the sound of knives, rifle butts, chains … Pablo emitted a rattling sound.

***

A woman in the cell wiped the blood from my face when I woke up. She said, "My name is Anna Kabiljo. I'm a doctor. They claimed I only helped people who sympathized with the president. That's why I'm here. I was raised in Argentina, but I am married to a Chilean. I haven't heard from him since the junta took him."

I repeated her name and looked in wonder at her pale but beautiful face. Anna Kabiljo. Kabiljo … Kabiljo … I said out loud. She looked at me suspiciously. Had I lost my mind? I squatted down and hid my face in my arms. Her last name echoed in my head. I'd heard it before, I thought. Then I raised my head and cried,

"Flora! She has the same surname as Flora! I'm not losing my mind."

***

Flora had only seen Anna once in her life, but she had told many stories about her "cousin in America."

Anna's parents sent packages to the family in Sarajevo. Once, Flora got a dress of tulle and a red-green quilted coat. She wore it all the time, even in summer, despite nearly fainting from the heat.

Anna's parents went from Yugoslavia to Argentina after the Second World War. Before the war, they had owned a jewelry store, but when the war ended, they had taken the jewelry with them and fled, terrified the communists would introduce the same political system as Stalin in Russia and seize their business. It wasn't long before the new authorities confiscated properties and imprisoned the owners.

On the way to Argentina, Anna and her family sailed to Italy first. On the ship, Anna's father recognized two guards from the concentration camp in Treblinka. One evening he almost strangled one of them on the deck.

Other passengers recognized men who had worked in other concentration camps.

Executioners and victims sailing together to the same destination. Anna's mother cried. Anna's father could not sleep. He smoked one cigarette after another.

***

Anna Kabiljo said that if I survived, I should try to find her husband and tell him she loved him. If she survived, she would find Pablo and pass on the same message.

It was five o'clock in the afternoon. I was waiting to be taken for questioning. A soldier ran in, grabbed my hand, pulled me to him, and told me to hurry. I couldn't walk, but he pulled me through a tunnel and into a long hallway. It stank of urine and excrement. He pushed me into a toilet and told me not to make a sound or move. He took the key out from the inside of the door, slammed it shut, and turned the key.

I squatted down and pressed my nostrils together with my fingers.

I must have fallen asleep. Woke up to knocking on the door. A beam of light blinded me for a split second. They're coming again, I thought. But a woman's voice called out for me to jump up on the toilet seat so they could break in the door. There was a bang, and the door opened. Two women and two men stood staring at me. They said they were from the International Red Cross. Anna Kabiljo had told them I was probably being kept hidden in a toilet. One of them wrote down my name and surname and asked how long I had been at the National Stadium. I replied that I didn't know and added, "Maybe a month."

They said I probably wouldn't be executed now because I was on a Red Cross list of prisoners. Then they left.

Two soldiers came, opened the cell, and took Anna.

I waited for her that evening. But she didn't come back. Not even the next day … ten days passed since they had taken her.

They took the skinny girl in the morning and brought her back a little before midnight. They pushed her into the cell, slammed the iron door, and locked it. The girl looked out with eyes full of pain, raised her head with difficulty, and said weakly, "They killed Anna … she died this afternoon. They locked her in a toilet. She died of food poisoning from her own shit."

***

A soldier stood outside the cell and pointed at me. I trudged out. He had to give me an important message. He said firmly, "Your children have been killed. If you want, you can see them, or rather their remains."

A woman from the cell yelled at him.

Three days later, the same soldier stood in front of the cell again, saying he had an important message. He told me that Pablo was alive. I looked at him. After a short pause, he said, "But we will kill him today."

I remained standing, but he pushed me into the cell. Some of the women lay unconscious on the floor.

***

I couldn't move my left arm. With my right hand, I felt a hole on the left side of my head. The blood had congealed.

A soldier stood over me, and when he saw I was

96

awake, he said, "You didn't succeed in taking your life this time. Let's hope you have better luck next time. You'd be doing us a favor. Leave our hands clean."

A nurse washed the blood off me. I was taken back to the cell.

***

My breath hung like a brown dwarf star somewhere in the universe. No one had caught the breath's danger signs. Only my father's words—*You need to educate yourselves, children*—rang out through the walls of the cell as absurd remnants of a distant, unreal time.

Images from his village, where Robert and I were sent on summer vacation, appeared in foggy whorls—fields heavy with tobacco, tall corn plants hiding corncobs, plump orange pumpkins, red juicy tomatoes … cows glaring with sad eyes, sheep wandering around with bells on their necks, grapes waiting to be picked, Sunday-best-clad young men and women who went to church only to gather outside afterward, after mass, in the hope of finding a companion for life.

Before I was taken for interrogation, I was allowed to speak on the phone with my mother. An employee at an office had presented himself as a friend of the family, so my mother thought I was at home.

She said she was no longer able to sew clothes. She began to sob. She mumbled that her life was over ... My father was the only man she had ever loved.

Then I knew he was dead. "His kidneys, which had been damaged during World War II, could do no more," she said more composedly. She couldn't imagine a life without him. Life made no sense. I said I would send a plane ticket so she could visit us.

The employee tugged my arm as a sign to end the conversation.

"Mom, I love you. See you," I said and hung up.

***

As if on a film screen, I saw Flora and me sitting at the table in Tilda's room a few months before she died. Tilda held her book and spoke slowly and clearly. "What I am going to read to you now, you must remember and use when times are difficult. You must repeat the words and think of the number *nine*. Words and numbers have great power and magic."

Tilda read, "Jesus said to the Samaritan woman: *A time is coming when people will not worship the Father,* neither on this mountain nor in Jerusalem. God is the Spirit, and those who worship Him must worship in the Spirit and in truth."

10

LORENZO AND THE SWEDISH AMBASSADOR

New patches of mold appeared on the gray wall. It stank of ammonia and damp. The cold of the cell settled in my bones. Sitting huddled together for warmth no longer helped. A woman who had blood under her nose began to shake. Then one with a broken arm. Next, a woman wearing only underwear. Dozens of women's bodies shook in time, mumbling.

I tried to escape with my thoughts. But I could recall neither images of my father's village nor Tilda's words.

I was woken up at two in the morning. A soldier said they wanted to talk to me. A frail woman got up and looked the soldier in the eye. "We know what that means. You want to torture her again. Haven't you had enough? She looks like a corpse."

The woman was slapped. I got one too before the soldier pushed me in front of him. He ushered me through a narrow passage and suddenly stopped. His blue eyes looked at me intently. The handsome features shone in the moonlight from a small round window in the roof. He spoke quickly and firmly. "Masha, don't you recognize me? It's Lorenzo. Your children are alive. They're with your in-laws. At the end of the corridor is a phone you can call from. Do it immediately and quickly. There's a shift change in five minutes. If the soldiers turn up, I'll have to beat you, so they think I'm interrogating you."

I didn't know whether I was dreaming, but I forced myself to think about where I knew him from. There had been a Lorenzo who was a member of Allende's party. He'd worked for Pablo. But what was he doing with Pinochet's soldiers?

I rushed to the phone and dialed the number. On the other end, I heard Rosalia's firm voice. I told her I was calling from the stadium and asked her to wake Alberto up. When he came to the receiver, I took a deep breath and said his dad and I were traveling for a while. He interrupted me. "Mom, I know everything. Can't you come back?"

I couldn't say more. A curious warmth flowed through my body. Was I about to faint?

Lorenzo signaled to end the conversation. On the way back to the cell, he slapped me a few times, so it looked as if I'd been beaten, and without moving his head, he said, "If you tell anyone, I will kill you."

Lorenzo came to get me again. He said a written order had come for my execution, but he'd torn it up before his superior had seen it.

Now I remembered Lorenzo. He'd visited us a few times while we lived in Santiago. He wasn't that well known in the party, but he was a good soldier, so the junta had taken him in. He was responsible for receiving the prisoners, and he tried to save as many as possible. And he was aware that someone, at some point or another, would expose him.

Lorenzo lived his double identity for six months, but because he was unmasked, he was executed in the middle of the *Estadio*.

***

I was weighed one morning at the end of December. When I placed my feet up on the scales, I glimpsed two numbers next to each other—eight and one. The display said eighty-one. But if you add eight and one together, that gives nine, I thought. And that was my lucky number! Could you be happy when you weighed eighty-one pounds?

The number nine now flashed brazenly in front of me. It was weird. I remembered the number nine stood for the prophets, like Tilda had said:

When people feel that a little kindness is worth more than dominion ... then there will be only one religion in the world, a universal religion.

It was a cold morning. I couldn't remember what the sun looked like, how it warmed. It was winter. A winter without snow, rain, or wind. A winter that was anonymous, faceless. I felt my heart pounding, but I didn't know why.

It was the morning that an unexpected guest showed up.

The guards called him a pig and a traitor. He didn't answer. They shoved and hit him. He refused to leave the stadium before they signed a document saying I would be released. It was the Swedish ambassador.

Rosalia had arrived with him. I was allowed to talk to her for five minutes. She told us that after we had been separated at the airport, the children were taken briefly to a juvenile detention center where they'd been locked up for two weeks until a prison officer showed up and smuggled them out. As it turned out, the officer knew Rafael, who had saved his life when he'd been hospitalized.

I asked why the Swedish ambassador was fighting to get me released. Rosalia said that Rafael had contacted many embassies. But the Swedish ambassador was the only one who'd reacted.

Now he was standing in front of me. Pinochet had no choice but to let me go. But only on one condition:

That I left Chile.

11
Alberto, Alma, and Augusto
Santiago, 1974

I was released on January 9, at eighteen minutes to nine in the evening.

It was common to release prisoners just before the nine o'clock curfew. If those released didn't make it home before then, the junta had an excuse for locking them back up.

Rafael's car was parked in front of the entrance when I came out. He accelerated and drove us home.

Rosalia opened the door. Alberto, Alma, and Augusto stood looking at me as if they doubted whether it was really their mother. Alberto said he knew they would release me before long. He had counted the days and was sure I would come home before one hundred days had passed. Alma asked why I was so skinny, and I replied that there wasn't much food where I had been. Augusto didn't say anything, instead he approached me carefully and offered me his hand. I seized it, pulled him to me, and held him in my arms as I struggled to hold back the tears.

I called my mother, told her the children and I were on our way to Sarajevo, and asked, "Can we stay with you for a while?"

"You're always welcome … I am so excited to see my grandchildren. I can't describe how much I've missed them all these years. Are you okay? I heard ugly things are happening in Chile."

"I've got a bad stomach bug, so I've lost a lot of weight. But don't worry. I just need a doctor."

***

In Sarajevo, I didn't talk to anyone about my time at the National Stadium in Santiago. I told Flora her cousin Anna saved my life, and she was executed later.

12

The Wedding Ring
Sarajevo, 1974

The slopes of the mountains were silent with frost, the streets muddy with melted snow and earth. The faces of passersby were red from the mercilessness of the cold. The sky was orange from the glowing embers of twilight. The few poplar trees and the suffocated flowers breathed sorrow. February was a tough month to get through.

The mailman's hands were stiff, his fingers pale and motionless. He dropped a letter in the mailbox and disappeared, unaware his snow tracks were following him.

I unlocked the door, ran down to the main entrance, and opened the mailbox. There was a thick brownish envelope. I picked it up. It was a little dirty. Under the postal stamps was an address: Ministry of National Defense, Chile.

I went up the stairs, closed the door, and held my breath. My hands were shaking. The knife I used to open the envelope shone with malaise. Out fell a watch, a ring, and a piece of paper. It was Pablo's obituary. His wedding ring was smeared with blood. Physical torture, I thought. They won't get me this time.

I got dressed and went out. Took the tram. Walked a bit. Came to a gray building. Handed the ring over and asked to have it analyzed.

A week later, the answer came. I opened the letter, unfolded a page and put on the ring. Sat down and read.

It *was* Pablo's blood.

13
TILDA
SARAJEVO, 1976–1978

I was no longer the girl my mother knew before I went to Chile. I had become withdrawn and serious, she said.

She had changed too. Couldn't bring herself to go out and visit anyone, neither her siblings nor her friends. Made up excuses to stay at home where her daily ritual was to sit quietly leafing through the album with photographs of my father. And she talked about Tito. She was worried about what would happen after his death. He had been ill for several years.

Robert and Kana had moved to Kana's hometown of Srebrenica. She wanted to live close to her mother and her sister. Once in a while we got a postcard on which Robert wrote they were doing well, but that he missed Sarajevo.

Space was a problem in my mother's apartment with two big and one small child as well as two adults. Alberto wanted to listen to loud music, and he and Alma didn't want to be in the same room as the youngest, Augusto. When Alberto couldn't stand being at home any longer, he went to a classmate's house after school. Alma didn't have any friends. She skipped school and sat reading at home. When my mother asked her if she should be in school, Alma said she had a stomachache or there was a flu epidemic at school.

I took her to a café to learn what was wrong. After we had talked for a long time, she admitted she was having trouble adjusting to the new environment. She missed Chile and her father. "I want to go back to Santiago. Everything is strange here. The people, the food, the weather. And I get teased when I speak, I'm not that good at the language, I mix Spanish words into it. Then they laugh at me. And the teachers don't say anything. Once a girl scolded the pupils in the class and said it was normal to mix languages when you move to a new country. She knew that because her father was a diplomat. Mom, I know you're good here in your home country, but think about me. And Alberto is having trouble here too. Let's go back."

I tried to hide how upset I was, but tears rolled down my cheeks. Alma began to cry too. We hugged each other. She begged me to move back … I dried my face and said, "I know it's hard for you and Alberto and for Augusto too, it's all so new. But I cannot go back to Chile with the political situation being the way it is. I'm not wanted there. I hope the situation will change one day. We have no choice but to stay here. I have experienced pain, but I'm letting it go, even though it's hard. We have to move on. We have to stick together."

Alma sat with a questioning look on her face. I continued in a confident voice. "Maybe you could invite the girl you mentioned over. I think you have a lot in common. And you can tell her about your friends in Chile. I'm sure she'd accept the invitation."

Alma's face lit up in a smile.

I held Alma's arm with my hand as we walked home. I felt like I had failed her, Alberto, and Augusto. Many times when I was with them physically, I wasn't there mentally, and now I could see I hadn't prepared them for our new life. It was as foreign to them as Chile had been to me when I'd moved from Sarajevo.

I have to make it up to them, I thought. I have to help them along. Otherwise, I'll lose them.

***

At three in the morning, I heard someone opening

the main door, going out, closing the door, and heading down the steps in the stairwell. My mother, who was sleeping in the same room as me, got up quickly, put her coat over her, and ran out. From the window, I could see her running after Alberto. A while later, a police officer called. "Comrade Masha, your mother and son are at the police station."

He handed the receiver to my mother. In a trembling voice, she said I should have told her about Alberto's sleepwalking. I explained that I didn't know he would sleepwalk again, as he'd been free of it for several years. But she kept repeating that I should have warned her and that it was such an unpleasant experience that she was afraid of having a heart attack. Her exaggeration irritated me, but I let it be.

My mother's anger only ceased a few months later when I was elected chairwoman of the local party association, a branch of the Communist Party. I had thought a lot about whether I wanted to stand for the position of chair. But I decided to say yes to it. Yes to having an influence on how society should develop. I was fed up with party members who wanted to profile themselves instead of getting important work duties done. Neither could I stand apparatchiks who used political phrases and convoluted bureaucratic language that most people couldn't understand. Plus, I wanted to realize my old dream of making the least well-off richer, so they could decide more over their destiny.

In the party association, we discussed what we could do to get more exhibitions, concerts, literary evenings, and a week's vacation by the sea. We established a fund, so those who had higher positions could give money to soup kitchens and school excursions.

***

My mother and the children were banned from the apartment for a few hours, so I could prepare my first speech to the local party association. I sat down at the desk and started flipping through some papers. But I quickly stopped.

It grew strangely quiet. A penetrating scent of quinces filled my nostrils. I felt a warm gust through the room. A quince on top of the closet fell to the floor. The bulb in the chandelier shattered. A light mist crept in through the window.

Flora's grandmother, Tilda, stood there wearing a long, white, see-through dress. Her face wore a tinge of melancholy. The eyes were blurry. She spoke slowly and weakly. "Masha, don't be afraid. I've come to help with Alberto's moonsickness. It can disappear completely. I will tell you how. Get my book and turn to page twelve."

"But I'm not allowed to read the book yet," I said, startled.

Tilda disappeared. Had I dreamed it? I was convinced I'd seen and heard Tilda, even though she had been dead for years.

I retrieved the book from a chest of drawers, but hesitated. Did I dare open it? Before I thought further, my fingers flicked to page twelve. There it was! The treatment: *Against all kinds of anxiety.*

I pushed the book away but a moment later picked it up again. Leafed to page twelve again and looked absent-mindedly at the text without reading it. What was I doing? Why should I do something I didn't really believe in and wasn't part of my life? Tilda had meant so much to me when I was a child, but now I was an adult and on my way to a new life. I didn't want to let the party down. Someone holding an important position within the party shouldn't believe anything resembling hocus-pocus, something not based on evidence and science. I couldn't understand why I was drawn to something so illogical. I had a weakness I would have to work on, I thought. But what if Tilda's recipe could help Alberto? Wasn't I willing to do anything for my children?

Alberto refused to follow the treatment. But I tried to convince him he should in order to get rid of his moonsickness. He called me a witch and couldn't understand how I had become superstitious. I explained it wasn't about superstition but about medicine that could make him better. "What will you say to your friends if they learn you go out at night on the streets and alleys without realizing it?" I asked, suggesting he could stop following Tilda's treatment if it hadn't helped in a few weeks. He promised to think about it.

He came home from school the next day and agreed to take the medicine, but only for two weeks and not one hour longer, as he put it. I mixed some herbs according to Tilda's recipe and set about making the magic tea.

At one point I asked myself what I was getting myself into.

I was forcing my child to do something that didn't seem like common sense. But it worked.

Alberto's sleepwalking stopped.

And it brought something else good with it. A woman answered my newspaper ad for an apartment to rent in the central part of the city, close to my mother. I looked at the apartment and said yes immediately. Now the children and I could start a new life for ourselves.

***

People sat drinking beer and chatting. The party association's rooms where I was to give my first speech were full of cigarette smoke and packed with people. Before I took to the podium, I went around and made conversation with people. Caught sight of a man playing chess, and as if he felt my gaze, he turned and looked at me. I felt I knew his turquoise eyes, close-cut blond hair, and Etruscan profile.

In the speech, I touched on the latest price increases, vaccination programs, and police reinforcements at football matches. When I finished, there were many questions.

A young mother, who had her child with her, demanded a smoking ban. The women voted for, the men against. The men were in the majority, and the proposal was rejected. The young mother left the meeting in protest, threatening to complain to the party leadership.

One man complained that the chairmanships didn't always go to the person with the most votes. "People with a certain nationality are elected as party chairman, regardless of whether they have a majority or not. That's unfair!" he said, agitated.

His words elicited boos, uncontrolled emotional outbursts, and vehement bickering. I stood powerless on the podium, not knowing how to cope with the situation. But out of the blue, I conjured up a TV image of the Soviet leader Nikita Khrushchev with a shoe in his hand. I bent down, took off a shoe, and banged it on the table.

Nikita's method worked. The noise stopped. There were whispers in a few places, but the eyes of those present were now directed at me. "Dear comrades. The different nationalities have lived together in Bosnia and Herzegovina for many centuries. And we will keep fighting for that to continue. But let's discuss the question of the election of party chair …"

I was interrupted by disgruntled shouts.

And thus ended my maiden political speech.

I got down from the podium and sat down at a table.

In a corner sat the man I'd noticed before the speech. He spotted me and shortly afterward approached my table and said, "I assume you want a *Sarajevsko*?"

I nodded. He fetched two glasses of beer. I asked what he thought of my speech. He looked at me like I was a little girl and said, "You're new to politics. There are things you probably don't yet know. Who do you think holds the most important positions in the police? Names that in eighty-five percent of cases belong to the same nationality. We are brought up to consider everyone equal. But there is a parallel society over which they rule."

His name was Anton. He wasn't a member of the party. He said firmly, "I do not wish to sell myself to an empty ideology."

14
ANTON
SARAJEVO, 1980–1984

The police superintendent gave instructions on what I, as a newly hired guide, was permitted to say and not say to tourists. I asked if it was really necessary, and he replied it's the duty of guides to care for our socialist country, especially now after Tito's death. There were many Westerners who were ready to undermine our unique system, the one we fought for during World War II, he said. He gave me the names of two people from a group of Austrian tourists whom I should keep a particular eye on. One of them was a former fighter pilot, and the Yugoslav intelligence service suspected him of being a spy. That day I had to show a group of Spanish tourists around too, and the police superintendent stressed I was to be aware of a woman who was related to Franco. I had to listen carefully to what the tourists asked and write a report about guests who behaved strangely and about those who wanted to know things beyond tourism.

The police superintendent summoned me to an "extraordinary meeting." He spoke slowly and clearly. A group of foreign journalists had turned up. They were on their way to the Serbian province of Kosovo where unrest was brewing between the Serbian police and Kosovar-Albanian students. "We will not allow them to enter Kosovo, will we?" he said. I was to have the honor of eating dinner with two journalists who were on the police's blacklist, so he added, "Make sure they have good food and plenty of wine. Use your feminine charm. And find out if …"

He didn't manage to finish the sentence. I got up, took my bag, and slammed the door behind me.

When I got home I called Anton. "Can we meet? I have to tell you about a meeting … I've changed my mind about the police. And, I quit my job as a guide."

***

There was a job as a Spanish and English translator at Anton's work. A furniture company whose administration building was in the city center. Anton was employed as an engineer.

I applied for the position. Shortly after, I got the job.

For Anton, working as an engineer didn't matter that much. He lived and breathed poetry and philosophy. Recited Sergei Yesenin and Federico García Lorca, sat for hours reading Søren Kierkegaard and Emanuel Swedenborg. We could learn from the philosophers' critical sense, control of emotions, and Christianity, as long as it wasn't linked to religious institutions. "We southerners are impulsive, rebellious, our blood boils. Nordic blood simmers on a low flame."

Anton and I had different views on politics and life in general. But there was something about his good-humoredness and handsome physique that moved me. How was he in bed? I smiled at my rhetorical question. I wanted to snuggle in, under his body.

We were to celebrate my new job at a restaurant in the old part of town with narrow cobbled streets.

A woman with luxurious blonde hair sang old Bosnian folk songs. Two men accompanied her. One played the harmonica, the other the clarinet.

We ordered the starter—cheese and smoked ham— and a bottle of red wine. The waiter uncorked the bottle and poured a little into my glass. I inhaled the ruby-colored liquid that smelled of wooden barrels and tasted of cranberries and walnuts.

A crowd of laughing men and women entered the restaurant and occupied the rest of the seats. They played in the Sarajevo Symphony Orchestra, Anton said. A younger pretty woman with combed-back brown hair smiled and waved to him.

She came up to us, looked at me, and said, "You need to know something. Anton doesn't have the raw mentality of our countrymen. His cultivated and sensitive soul can't thrive among "peasants" who don't care that he knows three foreign languages fluently and is a capable engineer. And he's not the type to fight for his rights, he almost doesn't care—"

Anton stopped her torrent by asking how she was. She didn't answer the question but mentioned she had just come from Vienna where the orchestra had played Tchaikovsky and Mahler, and where she had bought all the things that were in short supply in Yugoslavia—coffee, washing powder, and hairspray, which she had been making herself from sugarwater for several months. But now she had several years' supply of hairspray. She excused herself unexpectedly and went over to the others from the orchestra.

"She's a talented violinist," said Anton. "But she has problems controlling herself. She's reckless."

They had been a couple. She'd wanted children, but he wasn't ready. Wasn't sure if that was what he even wanted in life. And so, she'd left. It was as if something or someone was master over him, so he couldn't decide for himself. Now he could see that his doubts back then had been a good thing. "Children aren't for me, but it's good that you have children," he added.

We toasted. He took my hand, looked me in the eye, and said in a gentle voice, "I think I've been waiting for you. It took its time. But I'm happy now."

I asked if he wanted to live with me and the children. They had gotten to know him and liked him.

After a short pause, he said, "I would very much like to live with you and the children. But we have to get married first. I can't imagine living with the person I love without being married. I hope that's all right with you."

I nodded. He grabbed my face in his hands. Caressed my hair lightly. Kissed me and said, "You must meet my parents. And I will show you my horses."

***

During the school holidays, we went with Alma and Augusto to where Anton was born, a farm in the town of Lipik in Croatia. Alberto didn't come along. He would rather be with his girlfriend.

Anton's parents hugged and kissed their new grandchildren when we entered their house. His mother exclaimed excitedly, "Oh, I am so happy that we finally have grandchildren. They look sweet! I can't wait to hear all about you, children. Come with me, I want to show you something."

She showed them their chickens and pigs. Afterward, they went to an area with a lot of trees to see whether they could find any ripe fruit.

Anton and I went to the family's stud. A white horse came up to me and sniffed my hand. His name was Sirius. I patted his neck. He whinnied, stood still, and looked at me. I petted his forehead. He snorted hot air and sniffed my hand with his muzzle.

"It's a Lipizzan," Anton said proudly and continued, "They're one of the oldest horse breeds in Europe. They needed parade horses for the Habsburg court. By crossing European working horses with the more temperamental Arabian horses, they got Lipizzan horses. They're trained to perform difficult exercises and are known for their soaring jumps where they hang in the air."

Anton's mother set steaming food on the table—green beans in tomato sauce, roasted potatoes, bell peppers with garlic, two chickens, and a cheese tart. She fetched the region's mineral-rich spring water and Anton's father's homemade schnapps. We toasted.

***

At Christmas, Anton's mother, Alma, and Augusto decorated the Christmas tree. They attached cotton wool, long red candies wrapped in thin shiny paper in different colors, and glass baubles on the fresh branches and placed a star at the top.

Anton's mother served a roast from the farm's pigs, fried potatoes, stuffed cabbage leaves, and salad with boiled potatoes, carrots, eggs, and peas. And several variations of cake—dry, moist, round, square, with whipped cream, candied fruit, and marzipan.

After dinner, Alma showed me a sweater her new grandmother had knitted for her. Alma's face shone with happiness and her eyes smiled. "The sweater's green color suits my eyes perfectly. Mom, I am so

125

happy we're here. It's a lovely place and they're lovely, Anton's parents. Do you remember we once talked about how hard it was for me to get used to living here in Yugoslavia? I feel good now. I've made friends, I go to girl scouts, I'm doing well at school. I've really made an effort to do better and adapt."

In the evening, Anton and I were the last ones left in the living room. Heavily sated with food, I felt a tickling satisfaction. We tried to play cards, but instead, we drank ourselves to sleep on home-brewed wine.

In the morning, Anton's father and mother went to a market with the children. Anton and I went out to Sirius and the mare Silvia. They were already saddled, ready for a ride through woods and fields.

Sirius was slender with a slightly arched neck and muscular legs, and he moved his white body with majestic steps and dignity. He was a proud Lipizzan. At times I was frightened by his lively temperament, but his obedience surprised me.

***

There was a smell of quince when Anton and I entered his parents' house after several hours of traveling from Sarajevo. Out for the first time on our own, without

Alma and Augusto, who had stayed at home to spend the holidays with their friends.

The quinces were arranged in rows on cupboards and chests of drawers around the house. We sat down on a bench in front of a crackling wood-burning stove to get warm. The table was set, and we saw Anton's mother coming down the stairs from the first floor, smiling. She came to us with outstretched arms and welcomed us. Our winter vacation had begun.

The stove was still burning. I grew drowsy from the heat and told Anton I wanted to go out into the fresh air. The first star took its place in the sky, waiting to be admired down on Earth.

The trees shook off the snow as though it were scratching at their thin branches. The branches fell still and looked toward the sun-gray sky. A lark fluttered away from its hiding place in a tree canopy. It was as if the twilight bore pain due to the brief life of winter. Star after star began to fill the empty spaces in the sky, killing the snow. But no stars, not even Andromeda, could extinguish the disquiet that had crept into my heart with their light. I put my hand in the pocket of my winter coat and found something small and round. It was still there. The button from Niko's soldier uniform.

I was so happy my unease disappeared. The button was in the same place that I'd put it the previous winter. Before then, I had taken it out of the pocket of a dress I had worn almost all summer. "I've missed you, little friend," I whispered.

I heard Anton calling me from the house, but I couldn't move my feet. His steps approached in the darkness. When he caught sight of me, he was breathless. "You got a telegram from Sarajevo."

He took my hand, and we hurried back to the house. The telegram was from Robert. He had divorced and moved back to Sarajevo, Kana had stayed in Srebrenica with their two small children.

Robert wrote:

Mother is dead. Come immediately. Robert.

I rushed out. There was snow, piles of snow in front of me. I waded through it toward the car. Anton jogged after me, shouting, "Your bag!"

He put his foot on the accelerator. I made no sound. Anton wiped the tears away from my face with one hand and held the steering wheel with the other.

I would have told him about one particular morning

but couldn't. About that morning, before we left for Lipik when my mother had asked if what Alberto had said was true, that I had been held as a prisoner at the National Stadium in Santiago. She wanted to know why I hadn't told her about it. I replied that nothing had happened to me, but that Pablo had been tortured to death. My mother asked again what had happened and whether the soldiers had hurt me. No, I answered and explained that I only got a few slaps and that she shouldn't make a big deal out of it. But she threatened to write to the authorities in Chile to find out the truth. Or to Rafael, Pablo's father, who was now on his own after Rosalia's death. I told her I had lived in Rafael's house and that he had protected me and the children. She didn't believe me. She could sense that something terrible had happened and that I was lying to reassure her. She could feel my soul, which told her another story. She began to cry and threw herself into my arms. I held her without saying a word.

The Executive Council
Sarajevo, 1986

Stacks of documents about pine and beech trees, tree trunks, chairs, and bookcases took up more and more of my desk. I was tired of translating and wanted to quit the job and become what my mother had feared most—a stay-at-home housewife. I wanted to cook, clean, wash the dishes, listen to the radio, be with the children more. Test Alberto in anatomy and other subjects on his medical studies, and Alma in math—I could just about understand her high-school level. I could help Augusto, who was in the eighth grade, with physics. Or I could just sit and listen to what they had to say.

But I was worried about how we would manage financially if I stopped working. But then Anton came up with an idea. "If you feel you have to quit, then you do it. We'll be fine … I can give more lectures and earn more.

Little by little, my apartment became too small for the five of us. Alma thought her brothers took up too much room. Alberto got annoyed when Anton and I got up early. He and Augusto sought refuge with their friends and went to football and table tennis to avoid being at home.

Anton had pushed to get to the top of the list for one of the slightly larger apartments the company offered employees. But nothing happened. He was angry that party members were given the most coveted apartments, regardless of the size of their families.

We could no longer live on Anton's wages and his lectures, even if they were going well. We agreed I needed to go back to work.

I sent job applications, attended interviews, and inquired at various places. It was no use. Only when my replacement, the new chairman of the local party association, had spoken to his brother-in-law, who worked at the Executive Council, was there light. I got a job at the Council.

Universities and associations sent for Anton to present his lectures. He earned so much that he went part-time in the company and found time to finish an anthology of poems he had been working on for some time. When the collection was published, the Yugoslav Writers' Union offered him membership.

There, members could eat and drink, debate, chat, and read their texts.

Anton came home from a session at the Writers' Union. It was late in the evening. I had difficulty falling asleep, so I lay in bed reading a book. Anton lay down next to me and looked at me with lovesick eyes. He smelled of alcohol. Drunk again, I thought. I asked if he could stay home more in the evening.

Annoyed, he said, "*You* are the one who isn't home that much because of your career. And when we rarely talk, you're not truly present. It's like you're still dreaming of Pablo, waiting for him to show up. Or maybe you're dreaming of something else? I can no longer penetrate your world, Masha. I feel like a spare. Even the children have their own lives now."

I interrupted Anton. "Can't you see that you live in your own fantasy world with dead philosophers and poets? Look around and find out what is going on in your community instead!"

***

On my way home from work, I remembered I'd left the keys to the apartment at home. I headed to the Writers' Union to ask Anton for his keys.

He was sitting in the association's restaurant. The men were discussing women and politics and drinking wine. Anton offered me a glass. I sat down.

A man with a broad face and thick, shoulder-length hair that fell over his forehead in waves told stories from his village and boasted of having helped a young man achieve an exemption from military service. "I give them a piece of stamped paper with my name that states they are mentally ill. I can understand they want to avoid serving in the Communists' army. They should know their nationality and be proud of their forefathers who weren't poisoned by that so-called civilization."

The man looked at me and turned to Anton. "If your

beautiful wife doesn't know who I am, I will reveal the name from the afore-mentioned paper: Doctor of Psychiatry Radovan Karadžić, Koševo Hospital."

Radovan Karadžić wrote poems for children and adults in his spare time. For children about his grandmother and grandfather. For adults about the destructive power of the city and its imminent fall. The city was the most dangerous place on Earth, he said. It had to be burned, destroyed, razed to the ground. Radovan felt uncomfortable in its jungle. He had never been able to settle in it. "We have to get back to the mountains. Only there can we find love and happiness. Oh, my mountains, my valleys, my sheep, horses, and virgin women! Mountain people—these are true people! Not the lost souls in the concrete of the city. Civilization is destruction. It kills us with every day that passes. It takes our senses, judgment, dreams. Arise, my mountain people, my peasants! You are not the slaves of the factories, the oppressed of the red flag. You shall not betray your nation, your origin. Show us what you are capable of!"

17
PLANE TICKETS
SARAJEVO, 1990

Many went out onto the street to greet the first spring sun. Romany children sold little bouquets of hyacinths. The frost had disappeared.

Alma carried a bouquet of daffodils in her hand when she came home giggling from work. She had met the man for her dreams, she said. Kosta was his name. He had broken his leg and had been brought to the emergency room at Koševo Hospital where she worked as a nurse. They got talking, and it was as if they'd known each other all their lives. There was a special connection between them. She felt it in his eyes, which were deep, piercing. She knew having an intimate relationship with a patient was forbidden, but it was different with Kosta. They agreed to meet after he was discharged from the emergency room.

Three months later, they were married. Seven months later, they had a son. He was named Igor, after

Kosta's father. It was a tradition in his family. And Alma liked the name. She said it sounded like a balalaika.

***

The mailman knocked on the door. There was good news, he said, handing me a registered letter. He didn't want coffee, he'd had some at the upstairs neighbor. He hurried on.

When I opened the letter, there were two plane tickets for a Sarajevo-Santiago round trip. The tickets were from Chile's new government, which was going to unveil a memorial to Pablo.

The president, the Christian Democrat Patricio Aylwin, had set up *Verdad y Reconciliación*, the National Commission for Truth and Reconciliation to investigate the abuses committed under Pinochet. The commission concluded that at least 2,300 people had been killed or disappeared. President Aylwin apologized to the country.

I held the two plane tickets in my hand for a long time, teetering on the verge of tears with joy. Pablo had finally gotten his reparation. He deserved it, I thought.

Suddenly Alberto was standing next to me looking confused. I grabbed his hand and handed him a ticket.

Alberto, who had just graduated as a doctor, went with me to Santiago. For the first time since my expulsion in 1974.

18

His finger
Santiago, 1990

A civil servant from the Ministry of Foreign Affairs in Santiago asked if I was strong enough to hear how Pablo had been killed. I didn't have to decide immediately, he added.

Alberto tried to slow me down and said it wouldn't be good for me to hear it. But I insisted.

The official explained, "Your husband was locked inside the mine. He was mistreated for three months. He had written a letter to you and the children. He managed to give the letter to a woman who passed it on to someone else. In the end, it landed here with us. The woman later died in a mental hospital. She left a letter for Pablo too. I assume you should have them both."

The civil servant handed me the letters. I put the woman's letter in my pocket and opened the one from Pablo. He had seen me being mistreated at the *Estadio*.

The official continued. "Before Mr. Morena died, he was visited by a friend. The friend said that you and the children were still alive. Mr. Morena's last words were, *My wife and children are saved. Now I can die in peace.*"

After a pause, the civil servant said, "Your husband died a cruel death. They tore out his eyes and ripped off his nails and genitals. Then they tied dynamite around his waist and blew him up."

My legs began to shake under me. The walls of the office began to vibrate. The civil servant's head became two heads, and the family photos on his desk became black mirrors. I couldn't remember any more.

The official stood holding a glass of water when I came to. I asked what had happened. He held my hand and said, "You fainted. Drink some water and rest for a moment. I understand how you feel. It's gruesome. I hope you can handle it."

The only thing they found was one of Pablo's fingers with a wedding ring on it.

Desperation seized me at Pablo's fate. An unredeemed compassion gave a jolt through my body. If only I could bring Pablo back and hug him and hold him tight in my arms. Say that I still loved him, that my love was stronger than time and the blood of the executioners' hands.

***

Alberto tried to persuade me to leave the hotel in Santiago and go for a walk with him. I looked at him like I didn't know him. But he took my hand and pulled me up from the couch. He said we could look at the shops and see how much we could remember about the city. I got up without saying a word, and he helped me put on my jacket.

My hairdresser was still there, but several new hair salons and other businesses had opened. We walked in the direction of the parliament buildings. In one of the side streets, I stopped in front of a bookstore. In the window was a book about the coup. We went inside. I was shown the book and leafed through it. Alberto went to a bookcase to look at some other books. As I bought the book, I saw him talking to a young woman. I went over to them.

It was Isabella! Jorge and Maria's daughter, whom Alberto had played with as a child. She told us she was a qualified reflexologist and had her own clinic. Her father had disappeared on September 11, 1973. They hadn't heard from him since, but an acquaintance had seen him at the National Stadium. She no longer believed he was alive.

Alberto and Isabella exchanged childhood memories. Names of people and places tumbled out of their mouths. Light radiated from their eyes. Their voices crossed and melted into one. They almost threw themselves into each other's arms. In unison, they said how sorry they had been to say goodbye when we'd left for Sarajevo. They would never say goodbye again, Isabella said, and Alberto nodded, smiling. Suddenly they were holding hands.

The next morning I left for Sarajevo. Alberto stayed in Santiago.

A few months later, he wrote that he had a job at the hospital where Rafael, his grandfather, had once worked. Isabella and he had moved in together.

19
The letter
Sarajevo, 1990

I was sitting on the ottoman, looking at some papers I'd brought from work, when Anton came home from the Yugoslav Writers' Union around midnight. He'd had a row with Radovan Karadžić over his praise of the Russian writer and dissident Eduard Limonov. Anton had grown agitated that Karadžić praised Limonov's book about Pygmies taking over a city, wreaking havoc, raping women, and burning down the city. Anton looked me in the eye as he explained that these kinds of quotes and praise for nationalists contributed to dividing people and spreading hatred against certain nations. "I don't know how you and your party will stand against the nationalists, but are you aware that they come in all nationalities and infect like a disease? There are obviously more of them now than I had imagined, they are spreading like wildfire," he raged as his face turned red.

I could understand Anton. Some of us in the party knew what was going on and did what we could to combat what we termed hostile elements. The party had excluded several people with nationalist views, but

I wasn't sure whether the army supported our decision. It was as if someone in the party was pulling the strings without the rest of us being informed.

I told Anton not to be offended by it, and that he should think of his health. I was worried about him. He drank a lot, and I asked if he could do something about his drinking. Anton grew more agitated and yelled, "You obviously can't see what's going on in reality. Don't you understand that the socialist model has played itself out, that people can be greedy, power-hungry, and evil, regardless of the system in which they live, and that their urge to survive is greater than all the humanist ideas? Wake up and look around! The nationalists are winning in the polls. More and more people are joining their parties. Some people want it that way. They are creating this situation. It's happening somewhere out there, and I don't know what that is. You can't do anything about it, before it's too late, before it explodes. When you claim I drink too much, I have to ask how you are doing. Look at how you treat your children. Augusto always comes first. Alberto did too when he lived at home. But what about Alma? How many times has she asked if you could look after little Igor, but you don't have time because you have to see to your career!"

"You know what—I think you're jealous of all that

I've achieved in such a short time. And besides, my relationship with my children has nothing to do with you."

It wasn't the first time Anton reproached me for not being a good mother. Sometimes even I doubted whether I was fit to be a mother, but I couldn't stand the accusations any longer. I put on my coat and slammed the door. Hurried off like someone was after me. As if life was rushing away from me and I had to try to catch it. I paused for a moment. My stomach hurt. I waited for a moment, took a deep breath, and started walking again.

There was still light at Flora's. I rang the doorbell. She was going through her late husband's clothes to give them away. He had died two months earlier, and she said she might as well be doing something instead of tossing and turning in bed. She asked if I wanted coffee. I nodded. She headed into the kitchen. I sat down on the sofa, and when she came back with the coffee and two liqueurs, I told her Anton and I had had a fight and I needed to talk. I couldn't stand it any longer, I wanted a divorce. I said, "Whenever he's feeling bad he always takes it out on me. He believes everyone is against him, and it's all society's fault. In reality, he needs to catch up with the times. The only things he has in his head are books about dead writers and philosophers. I don't understand what he sees in their long-gone world."

But Flora could well understand Anton's urge to immerse himself in something meaningful. She believed we could learn from the past, and you couldn't separate the past from the present or the future. It was one and the same thing that flowed and moved back and forth all the time. Two steps forward and one step back …

I said I was afraid of what would happen to all of us and our community. Everything was changing so frighteningly fast. I wondered whether I should resign from the party. I no longer knew if what I was doing was good enough. Many had resigned from the Communist Party and had gone over to parties that divided the population according to nationality and religion. They must have been seduced.

I shouldn't worry, it was probably a passing phase, said Flora. "I think having several parties is healthy. There will always be people who abuse the system and line their pockets. And if I were to comment on you and

Anton, I think he's having a crisis. I think you should help him."

I said I couldn't help him if he didn't want help. He had to figure things out for himself.

Flora said I had changed.

"It's like you're not present when people are talking to you. I know it's been hard for you. You lost Pablo, were expelled from Chile … your mother died … your guilty conscience over leaving Niko … but you have to move on with your life. You don't know how long you have."

Flora's sermons and advice irritated me, so I changed the subject. I asked why she didn't want Tilda's book back. She no longer had epileptic seizures and was well now. She replied I should keep the book for a while longer, have some patience. She would work out whether it was best that she take it.

I got up, put on my coat, and opened the hall door. Flora said, "Maybe you and Anton should get a divorce. Sometimes that is what is best for both parties."

***

I took the dress off to wash it and heard something fall out of the pocket. There was a letter on the floor, and I picked it up. It was the letter I'd gotten from the civil servant in the Ministry of Foreign Affairs of Chile, written by the woman who knew Pablo. The thought I could have washed the letter with the dress scared me. Although I didn't know whether I was ready to hear more about Pablo's death, I sat down and started reading.

When I had read two-thirds of the letter, I threw it away and lay down on the floor, doubled over, and put my hands on my stomach to throw up. Yet I couldn't, so I tried to get up, but couldn't. Crawled to the phone and dialed Flora's number. When she answered, I tried to say something, but the receiver fell out of my hand, and I ended up on the floor again. Flora shouted into the phone, but I couldn't reach the receiver.

Flora came quickly and helped me onto the ottoman. Fetched a glass of water. She said she hadn't understood what I was talking about on the phone. All she could remember was something about a letter. She asked if Pablo was alive, but I told her he was dead.

I explained I had read a letter, and it had revealed something that broke my heart. Something I never thought Pablo would do. His life was his party, work, and family. I said, "I refuse to believe it's true. It has to be one of the junta's lies ..."

I took a deep breath and said, "The man I loved and trusted ... he ... he had a mistress. How could I have been so naïve?"

"How did you find out?" Flora asked.

"I read the woman's letter."

"Lots of men have a mistress, and women have lovers. It doesn't mean he didn't love you. My husband cheated on me once too. But I didn't want to divorce because of an affair. And it would have been a pity for Jasha, my only child too. Think about the good times you had together."

I grew angry and said, "The love between Pablo and I was special. You can't compare us to everyone else. You had to get married because you were pregnant, but Pablo and I knew we were meant to be together."

"Rubbish! Love develops through the years. It has nothing to do with sex but with understanding each other."

I felt a strong need to be alone and asked her to leave.

Flora put on her coat and slammed the door behind her.

I felt driven to go to the bookshelf and began frantically searching through the record collection. Very quickly I found what I was looking for. Vincenzo Bellini's opera, *Norma*. It had been years since I'd heard it. In Santiago. At the bottom of the cover, I recognized Pablo's handwriting:

To Masha, my love.

I put the record on and moved the needle to the aria, "Casta Diva." Went back to the ottoman, lay down, closed my eyes.

Maria Callas' voice flowed through my blood, my nerves, my muscles …

I saw Pablo surrounded by a fiery glow. He took my hand and held it firmly. More and more firmly … until the flames obliterated our bodies.

20

WE SUSPECT OUR CITY IS BEING MONITORED
SARAJEVO, 1991

It's a warm summer day without sun. In Slovenia, the Yugoslav People's Army fires on civilians. I discuss it with my party colleagues, with Anton, and with neighbors. We can't find out who is right—those who defend the army or those who fight against it. We believe the army wouldn't do anything wrong.

It's a wet day in August. The Croatian city of Vukovar is besieged by the Yugoslav People's Army and Serbian militias. I'm getting confused.

It's a Thursday in October. Dubrovnik is attacked by Serbian and Montenegrin forces. I'm getting even more confused. In Sarajevo we are confused. We still don't believe the army would do anything so wrong.

It's a blustery day in November. Anton's father is shot in his home. Silvia, Sirius, and the other horses from the stud die in a fire. Anton is hospitalized for a nervous breakdown.

It happens only 250 miles from our windows. Still, we suspect our city is being monitored. We're convinced a great city like Sarajevo won't be attacked. If a war comes, it will last three days at most, portends a neighbor.

The following year, the psychiatrist and poet Radovan Karadžić is appointed leader of the Serbs in Bosnia-Herzegovina. The police support the army and Karadžić's party. The few Croats and Muslims who have worked in the police form their own police force.

***

Robert's eyes were wide when he appeared with panic in his voice. "You need to escape! Buses are leaving the city. The Yugoslav People's Army is handing out weapons to the Serbian inhabitants."

His girlfriend, a Serb, nodded. She said her brothers had been given machine guns. I replied, "I don't believe in rumors. I'm not running away."

"These are not rumors," said Robert in a confident voice. He had seen the two machine guns himself. He considered fleeing. He wouldn't be forced to be a soldier, neither in the Serbian nor the Bosnian Army. "And petty criminal Muslims are busy procuring pistols from black market dealers. I have to go now. I'm going home to call Kana and the children and hear about the situation in Srebrenica."

***

Anton didn't feel like eating dinner when he came home from the psychiatric ward after his nervous breakdown. He didn't want to talk about how things had gone in the hospital either. All he said was that he wanted to come home. He sat down and turned on the television.

I sat down next to him, took his hand, and felt the warmth from his body. It felt like being in love with him again. "I'm sorry your father was killed. Losing him is terrible. I don't understand what is going on. And the horses were burned alive inside. How can anyone do such a thing?"

Anton kissed me on the cheek and said quietly, "It's good we're alive. One day I will establish a new stud farm."

He talked about us moving to his hometown and added, "I can no longer see any hope in Sarajevo."

"But there is still war in Croatia."

"Yes. But the Croatian army is approaching Lipik, and it will defend the area."

The TV showed images of despairing Croatian women, their bawling children, elderly people fleeing with bags and blankets, images of blood flowing.

21

He lay in the grass with a plum in his hand
Sarajevo, 1992

The snow had stuck to the ground. Not even the January wind could make it move. Instead it whizzed through the freezing trees on the other side of the street, causing them to shake.

Down in the yard was the noisy sound of meowing cats. A snowman stood alone with a scarf around its neck and two buttons for eyes, no nose.

The fierce ringing of the phone brought unrest to my mind. It had been a long time since Alma and I had spoken. Kosta, her husband, opposed the referendum on Bosnia and Herzegovina being an independent state, she said.

"I suggested we celebrate our independence from Yugoslavia. But Kosta was furious. He said he and other Serbs felt threatened and were, therefore, prepared to defend themselves when republic after republic chose to remain independent. They just wanted to remain in Yugoslavia."

Alma revealed that her life with Kosta was becoming more and more about politics, and on top of everything else, she was pregnant. I said she should think about the child and try to save the relationship, if nothing else, for the sake of the children. But it was difficult, she replied.

"I still love him, but he has changed a lot. He's almost never home and doesn't take care of Igor. He goes out and stays away for days without saying where he's been. And when he comes home, he's tired and dirty and reeks of alcohol."

"You could choose to think of the good in him."

Alma exploded, "You have no idea how bad our relationship has become! Can't you understand that? Get out of your bubble and look around. Tell me, do you still use the phrases *brotherhood and unity*? Do you still believe in the Communist Party?"

I fell silent. Alma hung up. My mouth went dry. I didn't understand how or why I and the party were responsible for her and Kosta's relationship and for what he did. Nationalism had existed before the Communist Party was formed ... perhaps Kosta had been indoctrinated. And perhaps he had been forced to do terrible things.

***

Many people were waiting in front of the bank that morning in March. I joined the line, prepared to wait a very long time. Thought about the referendum on March 1. I still doubted whether I had done the right thing. Like the majority of the population, I'd voted for Bosnia-Herzegovina to remain an independent state. But I didn't know how much being independent would help us. And I was afraid for the future. Serbian nationalists boycotted the vote and the declaration of independence.

I entered the bank and stood at the counter farthest from the entrance. I stood waiting for a while, and suddenly a deep male voice said in Serbian, "Away with you." I turned around and saw a man staggering. He was drunk and wore a dark uniform and black cap. He had long black hair and a long beard. He raised a gun from his belt and began shooting, first in the air, then around him. The bank's employees crawled beneath the counter. A bell began to ring. I crouched and hid behind a chair. The man stopped shooting and ran out of the bank. A woman lay on the floor. Her leg was bleeding. Dust sprinkled down from the bullet holes in the wall. The smell of gunpowder drifted through the door.

The church bells in Marijin Dvor in the central part of the city rang twelve times.

It was May 2, and I was on my way to work at the Executive Council. I thought of Anton. It was his birthday. I hadn't had time to wish him congratulations, he had already gone to work.

Sixty feet from the entrance to the tall and wide building where the Executive Council was housed, there was a sudden bang from the Vrbanja Bridge. A man yelled that I needed to hurry. "Can't you see they are shooting from the tanks! Our army, the Yugoslav People's Army, is shooting at us, at our city! They must have gone completely out of their minds," said the man, sobbing and running toward the Faculty of Humanities where a group of students were standing in front of the main entrance smoking, but they hurried in when they heard shots.

I stood still, not knowing whether to go forward or back. More shots were fired, and I ran into the Council building. The shooting continued. Shots were fired from the western side too. And from the north a little later. A handful of police officers moved into position and fired back from our building and from the parliament building next door.

A little after eight in the evening, I and four other employees had reached the eleventh floor. At that moment, a shell splinter flew through one of the windows. A young man was hit and dropped dead. More shots rang over our heads.

We hurried down to the tenth floor. Then to the ninth, eighth, seventh, sixth, fifth, fourth, third, second, first, ground. We paused and started to go up again. On my way up from the fifth to the sixth floor, the eighth floor collapsed, and I rushed down to the fifth … When I came down to the third, the fifth floor collapsed. I ran down to the second … first … ground. Only one man and I reached the basement.

I hadn't slept all night. Dawn heralded unrest. A shot in the distance. The man yelled, "Hurry! We need to get out of the building quickly."

He held out his hand and pulled me up. We went out. I looked up at the dark blue sky that was drowning in a long purple and orange streak. I had difficulty understanding what had happened. It must have been something I'd dreamed.

The man repeated our need to hurry. He took my hand, and we started running away from the building. A projectile bore into a tree close to us. We rushed into a stairwell. Through the window in the main door, we could see the remains of buildings and houses riddled with bullet holes. There was silence. We rushed out. There were deep holes from shrapnel in the asphalt. A tram was stopped on the tracks. The driver had been shot and was hanging over the steering wheel. Nothing moved.

The man whispered goodbye and headed north. I proceeded east. The main street stretched before me. I tried to avoid glass fragments … passed the body of a little girl with a toy monkey in her hand. I looked around … several dead. An old lady with a plastic bag in her hand. A boy with a schoolbag on his back. A man with broken glasses. A young woman who had lost a leg. The blood was still dripping from her leg …

An ambulance slowed down. A shot was fired. I ran away. Two shots were fired. One of them hit a tire of the ambulance. I ran faster and faster. Past shelled façades, burnt cars, smoke, the burning main post office. I ran but didn't know where to go.

The Executive Council moved to the Presidency Building, a mile farther east in the Bosnian-controlled area. Many of my Serbian colleagues had left the city. Most fled while others joined the Serbian forces on the nearby mountain to shoot at the city's inhabitants.

Several Muslims, who now called themselves Bosniaks, had gone over to the Bosnian side to defend the city.

Robert and his Serbian girlfriend were one of the few couples who flaunted their mixed nationalities. Initially they'd hid their love but grew tired of having to do so. They started going out together, and the first thing Robert said when he had to introduce her to friends and family was that she wasn't like the Serbs on the other side of the front line.

The terms Croats, Bosniaks, and Serbs now became common. Several months earlier, we were all Yugoslavs, and religion was considered something that happened behind the walls of the home, if it was at all practiced.

***

Anton and I were on our way to Flora's to celebrate the Jewish New Year, Rosh Hashanah, but on Tito's street, we were met with intense shooting between two groups of men. We couldn't get across to the opposite pavement. We turned, rushed back to the apartment and drew the curtains. Augusto had gone to see a fellow student. Lectures had been canceled, but the students carried on with their studies and sat the exam in the teachers' home.

I pulled the curtain aside a little. The neighbor's boy and a bunch of other children ran to a plum tree in a garden on the other side of the street. *Ah, no, they're not to go out into the street, they're good targets for snipers,* I thought as a feeling of anxiety coursed through my body. Maybe I should run up to the neighbor and tell her, her son was there. But my eyes were fixed on the boys. With quick movements, they began to pick the ripe plums. My mouth watered. I had only eaten a couple of dried figs for breakfast.

Anton was packing. He had to get up early. Off to the Bosnian Army. I asked if he was sure of his decision, but he had no doubts. He might as well do something sensible given he couldn't work anymore, he said. I was

161

about to tell him what was going on in the garden when there was a bang. I threw myself down on the floor and covered my ears with my hands.

I opened my eyes, got up, and ran out into the hall and up to the neighbor whose boy had been picking plums. Anton ran after me. I knocked on the door. Steps approached. The boy's mother opened the door. I told her where her son was. She raced to the window, and we hurried after her. When she saw what had happened, she started screaming. Her son lay in the grass with a plum in his hand.

The next day she sat under the plum tree, staring blankly out at the horizon.

***

Augusto stood in the doorway. He gasped and said, "They've shut off the gas! And the water!"

He asked what we were going to do and said he wasn't up for getting water. He was afraid to queue.

Before Anton joined the army, he was the one who fetched water. He went to a spring a few miles away in the old part of the city, and the place was one of the targets for snipers. So I left instead.

I zigzagged from sidewalk to sidewalk until I came to the spring that lay in a steep alley. Men and women with plastic bottles, buckets, and pots stood in a long line, shifting their balance from one leg to the other, swinging their containers impatiently. Two girls washed clothes. A young lad suddenly started shooting around wildly. The two girls ran away. An elderly gentleman said the man had grown nervous standing in a queue for so long. A woman and a man began arguing about who had arrived first. The woman hadn't eaten for several days, only a little nettle soup, she said, opining that she should be before him. But he hadn't eaten anything either, he said, and asked if she was aware there was a war and in war everyone was equal.

An hour after I had joined the line, it was my turn to draw water.

With quick, almost panicked movements, I put one and then the other canister under the jet of water, and when the canisters were full, I hurried as much as I could away from the queue. Now I was safe. I cheered. When I reached home, I experienced an otherworldly, almost religious, feeling of happiness.

Augusto embraced me and said in a weak voice, "I'm so happy to see you alive, Mom. I was terribly sad when you left. We mustn't part like that again. By the way, we have no more raisins and figs. Only three apples and five prunes."

I said encouragingly, "That should last us a few days. After that, I'll make lentil soup. For several days. If we get gas again."

Augusto made no reply but went into his room.

***

A hard rap on the door. I rushed over to open it. In front of me stood a woman. She said she worked for the World Health Organization and was distributing humanitarian aid. She handed over a package and said, "There's rice, brown beans, lentils, flour, sugar, and oil. It should last a month," she added and left.

Help came again the next month. There were preserves with fish, lentils, herb seeds, feta, and cookies. Augusto took a packet of cookies, looked at it, and showed me the date. The cookies had been produced in Great Britain in 1943. From the Second World War, Augusto snapped with a skeptical look in his eyes.

We didn't eat the cookies. Or the American ones, which were from the Vietnam War.

164

When the woman from the WHO came again, I asked why we got such old cookies. She replied, "There's nothing wrong with them, they're hermetically sealed. They keep as long as the package is unopened, and no oxygen gets in."

We didn't receive humanitarian aid for two months. I went to the nearby park and picked the few nettles and dandelions that were left. Put them in a basket, dug up some soil, put it in a cardboard box, and hurried off.

When I got home, there was gas again. I immediately set about making lentil soup, baking an herb tart, and making rice rolls from raspberry leaves. I put the soil from the park into two large cardboard boxes, put them out on the balcony, and sowed lettuce and parsley from the seeds in the humanitarian aid box.

The neighbor, Vanja, appeared and said her husband had shot a hare and she brought us some hare meat. We ate it with a little onion. There was one onion left. Enough for five days. A fifth each day. Augusto and I were lucky that day.

22

The same dream three times in a row
Sarajevo, 1993

Augusto slept for two days. Once he tried to lift his head and open his eyes but immediately fell back on the pillow and sank into a coma-like state. His girlfriend, Minka, had come to see what happened, but she didn't dare wake him.

On the third day, I shook him and told him I'd found some prunes.

He opened his eyes and looked as if he'd been awake for a long time and said, "The university is closed. We can't take our exams. Two of the teachers were killed. I've decided I will join the army. Better fighting than starving. I've already spoken with a superior."

I said I didn't care for him joining the Bosnian war.

"We still don't know who those people are. Someone saw foreigners wearing scarves with Arabic letters and religious symbols. They have nothing in common with the Muslims in Bosnia. You shall not fight alongside religious lunatics. You're risking getting killed. I don't want to lose you."

But Augusto emphasized he could also be killed on

the street or in the apartment. "I'd rather defend myself and my country. Many in the army there are Muslims, but there are also other nationalities—Croats, Serbs, and Jews. The officer I spoke to is a Serb … I'm fine with people from other countries helping us. What are the UN soldiers doing? Why don't they defend us, given that we can't have weapons? Our hands are tied. We can't do anything. The enemy in the mountains can see us, we can't see them. I can no longer be passive while my friends are being killed. Maybe Minka is right when she says we are just an experiment, that someone is testing us to find out how long modern humans can survive without food, water, and heat. To see how the civilian population reacts to incessant bombing. I'm sorry to say it, Mother, but you're still living in Tito's time. That time has passed. Can't you understand that?"

Augusto began to pack. I asked if he had spoken to Minka about his decision. She agreed and had even thought of following him and fighting, he said with an emphasis on "fighting." "But for the time being she will stay in Sarajevo."

Augusto put some clothes and a book in his rucksack, kissed me on the cheek, and left.

My thoughts were heavy, aggressive. Persistent. I obeyed them as I had once obeyed Pablo. Without condition, fanatically. One thought was present all the time. The thought of escaping. I imagined how I said goodbye to everyone I knew, how I simply disappeared. Away from the city where I'd been born, where I'd grown up. Flee from the remains of life, the last words of the dead, from fingers embedded in the rubble. From evil. Just escape.

I lay down on the ottoman. Closed my eyes, knowing I was prepared. Ready to fly away … it felt nice. I climbed higher and higher into the atmosphere. Through nitrogen, oxygen, water vapor. Reached where helium particles formed a light layer of air with sparkling dust, gases, and sulfur. It stank of egg. I saw winds caressing the sun. Vapors that removed consciousness, each at their own speed.

It was dark when I woke up. And soundless. I tried to get up but couldn't. I wanted to get a candle. Instead, I turned over on the ottoman.

I woke up again. My head was like a lead ball. It was night. Parts of a dream swirled in my subconscious.

I floated between sleeping and being awake. Opened my eyelids and saw a crack of light pushing through the curtain. I remembered the dream. It was the same dream I'd dreamed yesterday, the day before yesterday, three days in a row:

I return to Sarajevo from exile, but I can't enter the city. I try to move forward, but something is stopping me. I come to a house. I can't get in without jumping over the house. But as soon as I try to jump, the house disappears. I see another house. The residents won't let me in. They're after me. I hide. I jump on Sirius and ride into the house. I want to go home, my children are waiting for me, but I can't find the way out. The house now looks like the house we had in Chile, but Pablo isn't there. Sirius is no more either. I don't know how to get out. I spot a window.

Pablo stands outside and waits. He looks tired. He's hiding behind a large white shawl. I beg him to open the window and take me with him …

The candles cast a gloomy light on our faces. We sat with bowed heads. The mattresses stank of damp and cat pee. No one said anything. Once in a while, someone coughed. Suddenly, the basement door was flung open with a quick, powerful movement.

There stood Vanja, smiling. She looked at us and said cheerfully, "There you all are. How nice!" We lifted our heads, and she continued. "It's just like in the old days. People were good at enjoying themselves. They took their time. The cafés were full of musicians and writers reciting their poems. People drank coffee, smoked rolled cigarettes, and told stories." Vanja straightened as if she were about to announce a victory or some other piece of important news and stated in her deep voice, "Once a poet wanted to convince a group that there were no ugly women in the world. Then a woman, who had a flat, mostly misshapen nose, asked, *So, do you think I'm ugly?* "He replied, *Not at all. Every woman is an angel who has fallen from heaven. Even you. But you were a tad unfortunate and landed on your nose, mushing it a little. It doesn't matter in the slightest.*" Vanja laughed aloud.

She quickly moved on to another subject as if she had limited time for her performance. "I'd now like to recite a sonnet written by the great Shakespeare."

She recited not just one, but five sonnets, in English. Most people didn't understand a word of it. Yet they gazed at her as though she were speaking in a magical language that brought them happiness. I began shivering with cold as I wondered whether I was freezing to death.

Vanja was a former high school English teacher. Her husband had lost a leg when a grenade hit a line of people queueing for bread. When she was told, she ran up and down the stairs in the stairwell, shouting, "Will they continue to claim that *we* threw the grenade ourselves, that we are masochists, beasts from the Balkans? We are stronger than them. Even without tanks and rockets!"

Vanja shouted and shouted. Eventually she grew tired, so she sat down on the stairs and sobbed. "What am I doing in this damned country? How can I provide for a one-legged man?"

Mira, another neighbor, got up and announced that she too liked poetry. Her husband interrupted her, saying proudly, "She even recites poems when the bombs are falling. Once she drowned out the sound of the grenades."

He took the stage. "Recently I started wondering how many times in my life I've tied my shoelaces. When I worked it out at long last, I almost wanted to take my own life."

Mira added, "He couldn't handle the high number."

I couldn't understand it had taken a war for me to get to know these people, people I'd only known superficially. Now they stood before me, defying bombs and misery with their laughter and pride. And I sat warming myself with their humor and courage, hoping I would feel better.

Adi, who was sitting next to me, got up impatiently. "Be quiet. I want to sleep. I have to get up early. I have to chop down a tree for firewood. Have you ever tried making tea from a tree root? It warms you up."

Adi looked after the nearest park with his dog and his parrot. He tied the dog and the parrot to a fence, mowed the grass, and removed dog shit from the paths, even while the snipers were shooting from all sides as if he didn't hear or see anything. His eyes seemed to see the beyond where no one but him could see.

When he wasn't doing his volunteer work, he jogged. He ran in a red T-shirt and yellow shorts, even when it was fifty degrees Fahrenheit. Once I asked him where he ran. He didn't answer, just ran even faster. Through streets, graveyards, over hedges. He hastened off as if at the end of the run, he would be received by beautiful and eternally young women. When he came back, he ran up the stairs and knocked on my door. At first, I was afraid of him, but later I realized he meant me no harm, and he lived in a world that was both mysterious and terrifying.

Occasionally he would ask for a few pennies for food. Afterward he would tell me another story about creatures I'd only heard about in fairy tales. "Once I heard a fairy sing. I'll never forget her voice. Fairies live in the clouds where they build castles, they live in forests, on water, on stars. Mountain fairies go into caves and turn into snakes. They are psychic, they can bring the dead back to life and heal the sick. When fairies get angry, they get their vengeance, shooting arrows, wounding, and killing. They raise storms at sea and destroy dinghies and ships. People go blind if they hear their song or see them bathe naked."

It was Tuesday. I was on my way to Flora's when Adi came running by. He stopped abruptly when he saw a young girl with long red hair. Her miniskirt had caught his eye. Both she and her makeup were beautiful. Her sheer tights revealed long ivory legs. The girl stood between two grenade holes in the sidewalk, looking like a statue that had been gracing the street for hundreds of years. Adi stared at her admiringly. "Will you marry me, beautiful girl? I have been waiting for you for years, and now I have finally found you. I will bring you happiness. If you say no, you will be unhappy for the rest of your life."

As though frightened, the girl retreated a step, but when she looked at Adi again, she started to laugh. Her laughter was so loud it confused him, and he began to stamp the ground like a rooster ready to fight as people crowded around him and the girl.

Glaring at her, he said, "What is it that you don't like about me? Do you think I'm a madman? Did someone tell you that? I know what I want. I want you. What's wrong with that? With me, you will be a princess. I only want to live for you, breathe for you, run for you, eat for you, defend you, carry you on my back … You shall be mine. I've seen it in the old fortune teller's cards. If you don't marry me, you will be killed within four months.

Do what I say, I beg you. You must listen to your fate!"

The initial reaction of the bystanders was one of laughter. Then they scolded Adi and told him to get lost and leave the girl alone. The girl said nothing but turned her back on him and left.

A month later she was killed by a sniper. Just a few yards from where she'd met Adi that Tuesday.

***

It had snowed all night. The streets were empty. No cars. In the afternoon, Robert turned up with a wood-burning stove.

His company had been hit by grenades and so had closed. Subsequently he had started making stoves out of tin from drainpipes.

Robert went into the living room. Vanja was with me and sat knitting. When she saw the stove, she immediately went out to tell the other residents the news.

They brought newspapers, paper, cardboard. Mira brought stacks of books on Tito and Lenin. When she set it alight, her eyes shone with delight. "They lied about their communism and lined their own pockets. There's no socialism in real life. Oh, how stupid we've been."

I couldn't resist interfering. "Perfect countries *don't* exist. Yugoslav socialism has had many positive sides. We've lived together for hundreds of years, and now we are to be divided on the basis of religion and nationality.

"There will come a time when we will miss Tito and the privileges we had then. Free education, health care, and the workers who, despite being apparatchiks, were able to decide what was to happen to their company."

I was surprised that so many people could change their minds so quickly. Yesterday they were ardent Communists enjoying the benefits of the system. Now they didn't want to be associated with it and considered it their worst enemy.

Robert had heard from Kana, he said, when the neighbors had gone. General Morillon had declared Srebrenica a UN-protected zone. They were lucky, added Robert. Kana and the children now lived with her mother. Her sister had moved home too. He said Kana was sorry she had bothered me with her many calls when I lived in Chile. I asked why Kana was thinking about it now. He believed she had changed because of the war.

Robert chopped the double bed to pieces, tore up part of the parquet floor in the hallway, and put it in the stove. I started to sweat. Robert walked around to see if there was more he could throw into the fire. He came out of the bedroom with a stack of postcards and said, "More for the fire? You have so many!"

There were over 350 postcards from different places in the world. I flipped through the postcards quickly and removed one. I handed the rest to Robert. They were added to the blaze and swallowed by the flames.

Robert asked about the postcard I didn't want to part with. It was from a Greek. I explained, "I met him by the Adriatic Sea the summer I was sixteen. We were chatting on our way to the beach when he suddenly stopped. Without saying anything, he embraced me, held me tightly in his arms, and kissed me. A long, passionate kiss. He traveled home the next day. I never saw him again. But I never forgot my first kiss."

***

The door was open. Vanja stepped inside, pale and

staring straight ahead. Didn't say anything but handed me a piece of paper. Then went.

I read what she had written:

You old Europe,

You say we are Balkans. That we are, but we still belong to you.

You say you don't want borders, but you allow borders around us, in our cities, villages, neighborhoods, apartments, in our minds.

So many dead, wounded, homeless.

I laugh no more, cry no more, speak no more.

But I remember.

Vanja turned up again the next day. First, she cried. Then she screamed, "Masha, evil is upon us! Even my cousin has betrayed me and my family. He's an executioner in a concentration camp! The one who's a professor at the university. How could that happen? Had he become bedazzled all of a sudden one day? Or had he always hidden his hatred for people of other nationalities?"

I didn't believe her words. But in a melancholy voice, Vanja said, "My cousin was recognized ... and our neighbor, Mira's husband, was recognized too! I thought he'd been killed when he disappeared a while ago. But he apparently turned into a sniper who, with the help of a rifle with a scope, shoots at people."

The electricity had come back on. I invited Vanja and her husband for coffee, which I'd gotten from Alberto and Isabella. They had also sent me cakes, laundry detergent, soap, and shampoo. In a letter written in Spanish included in the package, Alberto asked whether I'd received the other six letters and packages from Santiago. *Where* had those packages ended up, and who might have eaten the contents?

When we finished drinking coffee and eating cakes, I turned on the transistor radio. Pop music played. Vanja and her husband immediately began moving their bodies. Her standing up and him rolling in his wheelchair. The joy in their eyes made me jump up and dance with them. Our spontaneous movements melted with the healing notes …

***

I went down into the basement, despite no shells falling that day. Sat on a chair. Closed my eyes. The silence welcomed me. I grew scared.

I started when a rat scratched the window. I tried to let go of the anxiety, but a bird began to circle under the ceiling with a ringing, flapping sound.

I wanted to forgive. I just didn't know who and why.

Instead, I got up and went out into the street. Saw my shadow. The moon insisted on shining its light on me without asking permission. I heard my grandmother's voice:

They can take everything from you, but they cannot take your fate.

***

Augusto's girlfriend, Minka, was happy that Monday. In three days, Augusto would get leave from the army and come to visit. She didn't know how long, but last time he stayed with her for seven nights. With just one day, he could make her happy. One day of touching, when she could feel alive.

Minka was happy that Wednesday. Only one night left before Augusto got leave. But there was no more water left in the canister. So she and a friend took two canisters each and went to fetch water.

At the Music Conservatory, they turned down a side

street. Just then, a cartridge flew through her friend's up-do and hit Minka in the head. She collapsed.

An ambulance came and she was taken to the hospital. She had lost a lot of blood. The hole was deep.

Minka died two hours after she was hit. By a sniper. She was just twenty-three years old.

The friend said that Minka and Augusto were to have been married two days later.

The same day Minka was killed, Augusto dreamed a sniper would kill her. "At first I didn't want to believe it. You know I'm not superstitious. But now I can see a connection."

He could remember the sniper's name. He'd seen it in the dream. "The name was written on a wall. I get goosebumps thinking about it …"

"Is it hard to say the murderer's name?" I asked.

He said, "It's our neighbor's husband! Mira's husband. That was his name. I saw it in the dream."

Augusto refused to see other people. After two weeks, he went back to the front.

***

Alma started looking for Kosta, her husband. She visited friends and acquaintances. She looked for him in streets and alleys, in parks, at humanitarian organizations, in morgues, and in the Serbian Orthodox Church. He had become a believer and joined the church with the only Serbian priest left in the city. But the priest had not seen him in a while.

Eventually she gave up and began getting used to the idea that he might not be alive.

Alma's children, Igor and Veronika, sat on the doormat in front of my apartment crying. Alma was leaning against the railing, trying to comfort them when I got home. Alma was quite thin. You could see her cheekbones. I asked what had happened. She sighed and said a shell had destroyed their apartment. "We could have been killed. We were eating in the living room when we heard a bang. We hid under the table. When we got up, we were white with dust. Only there, where we'd been eating, wasn't hit. The rest of the apartment is in ruins. It's a miracle we're alive."

Three-year-old Igor had peed the bed again. Alma couldn't wash his sheets. There was no more water, so she just hung the sheet up in the bathroom. Igor started crying and said he wanted to go back to their apartment to get his toys and his father.

Veronika, who was almost two, didn't say much but sat playing with her doll. She refused to eat, but when Alma told her a story while holding a piece of a cookie in her hand, she began to eat a little. And when she and Igor found a playmate, a five-year-old girl from next door, she ate almost everything that was served.

The girl and Igor played soldiers with machine guns while Veronika tried to join in. Igor said he was afraid of grenades. The girl reassured him and told him not to be afraid as her father wasn't going to vacuum that day.

Augusto, who was visiting, thought it sounded suspicious.

He contacted the police, who investigated the family's apartment. They found the vacuum cleaner and in it a radio connection. The girl's father was collaborating with the Chetniks, sending signals to them when children were playing in the street. So they knew when to shoot.

***

Flora dropped by unexpectedly, walked into the

living room with a sigh, and sat down on the ottoman. She looked tired. The bags under her eyes dominated her face as she looked around with sunken eyelids. Trembling, she said, "Something terrible has happened."

Her son, Jasha, had gone out to get water and his wife had gone out to scrounge food. Their little daughter, Erna, had stayed at home playing with a girl whose mother was taking care of them.

The girls had been sitting, playing with dolls when a grenade exploded. Two walls and the ceiling in the living room had collapsed. Dust and smoke spread everywhere. Furniture, windows, and fragments of glass flew through the air. The girl's mother pushed her way through the remains of the walls. Erna lay in the middle of the room covered in dust. She opened her eyes and said she had a stomachache. The girl's mother wiped dust from Erna's face, picked her up, laid her on the floor in the hall, and said she would come back. She looked around, spotted her daughter's legs, and ran to the door of the living room. The girl's body lay between broken bricks and plaster. She was holding a doll in her hand ... but her head was gone ... It was by the window.

It happened in the morning. That afternoon the girl

was to be buried. It rained heavily. But the moment her coffin was lowered into the ground, the rain stopped. "It was a good sign," said Flora. "If it rains during a funeral, it means misfortune. When the coffin was covered with earth, the heavens opened again, and the rain poured down."

Jasha and his wife and little Erna moved in with Flora. Erna developed a stutter and no longer played with other children.

***

A few days later, Flora came by again, saying she needed to find a recipe in Tilda's book.

She flipped through the book as if she knew where the recipe was. When she found it and wrote it down, she said, "It will help Erna."

I asked her why she didn't take Tilda's book with her. It was Flora who was supposed to have it. She replied, "It doesn't matter if it's you or me who has the book. To Tilda, you were a granddaughter. We don't know which of us two will survive the war. I just feel that you should have the book."

I wanted to ask Flora why I couldn't open it until after she was dead. I wanted to tell her that I had been in contact with Tilda's spirit and I had looked in the book, but instead I asked, "Who was the old woman with you when I came to say goodbye, before Pablo and I went to Santiago? She left quite an impression when she told my future. I didn't believe her prediction that Pablo and I would divorce. But she was right. Pablo's life ended tragically, and that's how we divorced. I went through so much when I lived in Chile, and now I've lost faith in people and in a better world. I'm in despair. And the war keeps going. No one knows when it will end. Dark thoughts fill my head more and more. Thoughts of my nearest and dearest dying. Those thoughts haunt me. At the beginning of the war, I hoped the nightmare would soon be over. But now that hope is gone. I'm afraid. Afraid of everything. Of the anxiety … I'm not able to work anymore … I can't sleep … I can't fight either … Augusto wants me to leave, but I can't decide. I no longer know what is good and what is bad for me. I can no longer feel my intuition, I've lost my will … I could flee the city when the WHO returns in a few days. Augusto knows a woman who works in the organization. I need to figure out what I want soon. Stay or flee."

Flora didn't answer my questions about the fortune teller, neither did she comment on my situation, but asked if I'd heard from Anton.

I replied, "No one has seen him for a long time. I've asked many people. It's strange, but I don't miss him. Don't know why I feel like this. You're lucky your husband died before the war."

"Perhaps. But you're the lucky one. You did what was right for you before you married Pablo, and he gave you everything. And Anton loved you and spent a lot of time with your children while you were engrossed in politics. You didn't do much to save your relationship."

"What do you mean I didn't do much for our relationship? You know very well I could do nothing about his melancholy. He refused to do anything about it. Instead, he started drinking and spending more and more time at the Writers' Union … and of course he likes my children. I raised them well. They have managed well despite their turbulent life. Anton couldn't have children himself, and he was happy to take on my children. You sound jealous of what I've achieved. You didn't bother to get involved politically, you didn't care how society was developing. You were just your husband's cook, laundress, and nanny. You never talked about how things were in the bedroom … I don't think we should talk about our marriages. Won't you tell me who the old woman was?"

"What woman?"

"The one with the long white hair. She told my fortune with white beans. Alberto was four months old at the time. I stopped by to say goodbye because we were leaving for Santiago."

"Oh, her. She was someone Tilda knew. I don't know if she's still alive."

"Why did she have to tell my fortune?"

"You ask too much. It happened years ago. I don't remember what happened that particular day."

Flora said no more. She took her bag and left.

***

The cold had crept into the walls. There was no more firewood. I was swaddled in a blanket, and Veronika was wrapped in two blankets and playing with her doll. Alma and Igor were visiting Robert. He needed to be comforted, Alma felt. His girlfriend had left him and gone to Serbia.

In the afternoon, Vanja came inside wearing a thin coat and holding a plastic bag. She had developed prominent cheekbones and pale lips. With careful movements, she took a package out of the bag and placed it on the table. She unwrapped it and said loudly,

"This is for you!"

I went to the table. A dark red and gunky mass stuck out of the paper. It looked like something I had seen a long time ago. It can't be meat, I thought. I took it in my hand, turned it this way and that. Felt it, smelled it. Looked suspiciously at it and asked, "Is it really meat?"

"It's meat!" said Vanja excitedly.

"Have I gone mad? I don't recognize it."

Two pounds of meat cost 50 Deutschmarks. Vanja must have given the last of her money for the small chunk of meat she'd bought on the black market. I was so touched. She looked like an angel, and I regretted thinking of her and the other neighbors as opportunists the other day. She stood before me, and I realized it wasn't meat she held in her hand but her heart.

She explained, "I've decided to enjoy life. I don't know if I'll be killed tomorrow. From now on I will find something encouraging every day. Do you realize we can't figure out how to enjoy life? We live to survive. But the war has taught me to enjoy being. When I get dressed, when I chat to other people, and when I listen to the grenades. I've learned to be grateful. For a flower, a spoonful of soup ..."

Before saying goodbye, she said, "In reality, the bombs are heralding a new and better time."

I went out of the living room. Before I reached the kitchen to see whether the gas had come back, there was a bang. I rushed to Veronika, took her in my arms. Another grenade exploded in the apartment below us. Shrapnel ricocheted through their bathroom and hit the downpipe on our toilet.

I went in to see Vanja. Her toilet was destroyed too. And all the other toilets in the house.

We relieved ourselves in plastic bags, which we threw into the overflowing dumpsters.

The stench from the containers spread, penetrating the apartments.

The authorities ordered that the waste be burned. But the fear of snipers and grenades was greater.

Two months later, Robert obtained some material for new pipes and repaired the toilets. But the stench lingered.

***

There was a bag of raisins and a tin of chickpeas left. We could no longer count on getting humanitarian aid. The children's bodies grew thinner and thinner. Their movements slower. I wanted to cry. But I held back the tears.

Alma's hair had developed a gray tinge, her sunken face had wrinkles and a greenish color. The sparkle of her eyes had disappeared, replaced by a dull expression. It scared me. She was unwell and paced back and forth from room to room to figure out if she and the children should leave. Igor screamed every time he heard a shot.

Someone knocked on the door. I opened it, and there was Augusto, tall and out of breath. He said there were a few seats left on a WHO bus going to Split as part of a convoy. Alma didn't hesitate any longer. It was as if she had been waiting for this message.

She packed some clothes in a bag, put a teddy bear and a doll in it, told Igor and Veronika they were leaving and to say goodbye to me. Igor said he would miss me. Alma said they would come back when no more bombs and grenades fell. Igor asked if they could get his toys, but Alma replied that their apartment was destroyed, and it was too dangerous to search for toys. Veronika gave me a hug and asked why I wasn't coming. I said I'd like to, but that I had to look after the apartment. Alma hugged me and said we should promise to see each other soon, no matter where we found ourselves. I nodded and wished them a safe journey and told them to write or call if there was an operating telephone. A tear ran down Alma's cheek. She dried it and turned to the children.

Augusto followed. They walked. I closed the door and stood listening to their footsteps. Silence fell. I opened the door. They were gone. The smell of Nivea cream, which Alma used on herself and the children, lingered in the hallway. I ran down, but Augusto's military car was no longer there.

24
FLORA

On Saturday, February 5, Vanja got up early to go to the market. She had heard you could buy cheese tarts.

I got dizzy and lay down on the ottoman. The wind whistled outside the window and pushed the branches of the poplar tree. A quince on the wardrobe rolled and fell to the floor.

I got up suddenly as if pushed from behind and pulled to the window. I started scouting from house to house, from apartment to apartment. When I reached the last window, something inside me snapped.

I looked around the living room and spotted Flora's picture, which was hanging a little askew. I straightened it. It was a picture I took when she'd received a music award for her piano playing. Her face shone. I couldn't remember when it was. But I remembered what she played: *Valses nobles et sentimentales* by Maurice Ravel.

At one o'clock I turned on the transistor radio. There was only one news headline. The studio host named a market and a massacre. Many dead and wounded.

I heard the opening sentences, and my legs went out from under me. My left arm became heavy and lifeless. I don't know if I fell or disappeared, but it felt like I was detaching from my body and began circling in the air. Far, far away I heard the radio playing sorrowful music. I watched time go by for a long time—seconds, minutes, hours.

It was dark. I felt the cold from the floor. It made me shudder. A human silhouette stood in the door frame. The silhouette ran toward me. Two hands lifted me up. A candle was lit. I saw a face and eyes that met mine in the same prism of light. The eyes were so intense I was scared. I screamed. Threw myself into Vanja's arms. Our faces crashed into each other. Tears rolled down our cheeks and I exclaimed, "I'm so happy you're alive!"

She stammered, "It's horrible … the cruelest thing I've ever seen … and … I … I have to tell you …"

Vanja said that she had gone to the market, but the cheese tarts were far too expensive, so she'd left again. After she had walked a few hundred yards, the asphalt suddenly cracked under her feet and an explosion echoed through the streets. A few seconds later, she heard a loud noise. She ran back to the market where a terrible sight met her:

Mutilated bodies, last breaths … Survivors calling for help. Some people get up. They see the mutilated bodies, stagger, collapse. Sirens sound …

The first ambulances arrive. Paramedics and bystanders put the dead in potato sacks and black plastic bags. Cars stop. Drivers and passengers run out and search for survivors. The aluminum bars from the dismantled stalls are used for stretchers. The wounded are helped into cars.

Covered in blood, people move from one booth to another, from one torn body to another. Ambulances depart, sirens blaring. A cavalcade of vans, trucks, and passenger cars bear the dead and wounded away.

The street transforms into a hill of blood. People walk around with horrified looks, asking, Is the florist alive? Does anyone know what happened to the man at the vegetable stall? Have you seen a woman with a blue coat, she sold coffee?

Their questions are drowned out by the noise of traffic and moaning. The goods and wares from the destroyed booths lie pell-mell—crushed canning jars, dried flowers, jeans, little herb bags.

Two UN vehicles pass without stopping.

Vanja stopped talking. She gasped for breath and then continued in a low voice:

She … She lay on the asphalt … Flora … Next to her sat an old lady holding something shiny that rested on her knee … Two men came, they lifted Flora's body and placed it in a dark car. I asked the old lady what had happened.

She said:

Flora and I arrived at the market together. I wanted to buy sauerkraut, so I went to a stall with cabbage. Flora went over to the opposite side to buy a cheese tart. Suddenly the whole square shook. I was thrown toward the supermarket, crashed through the door, and fell to the floor. I have no idea how long I lay there, unconscious, but I came to when a young woman called for her child. I felt a wound on my head. A man helped me up and took me to the hospital. There was blood everywhere. The hospital looked like a slaughterhouse. I waited for a long time and couldn't take it anymore. I tied a scarf around my head and went back to the market to look for Flora …

***

Flora could not be buried at the Jewish cemetery on the other side of the river as it was the front line between the Bosnian Army and Serbian forces. We had to find a plot in the city's large graveyard.

The plots stood ominously close and looked like white moonstones on a lifeless globe. The trodden paths and grenade holes formed little puddles of ice.

When we found a small vacant plot, Flora's son Jasha and his friend quickly dug a hole, laid Flora's corpse wrapped in a shroud into the grave, and covered it with the damp earth. I put a few plastic flowers on the grave. Jasha grabbed me by the arm and mumbled that we should hurry out, there were snipers nearby. We hurried out of the cemetery. Jasha's friend said goodbye and we ran across the street and into a stairwell. The window was broken, and a draft came from above as if the house were hollow. It looked abandoned. Jasha said he had to go home, but he wanted to give me something before he left.

He stuck his hand in his coat, took a piece of paper out of his pocket, handed it to me and said, "My mother wrote a poem a few days ago. As if she knew she was about to die. It was the first time I saw her write a poem. She wouldn't show it to me but said you should have it."

I unfolded the piece of paper and read the poem …

looked at the poem and read it again. But I didn't know if I understood it and said to Jasha, "I didn't know she wrote poetry either ... It's like the poem is in code."

"My mother's humor fluctuated a lot lately. She talked about Tilda and you. And about a book. I didn't understand much of it, but I remember she found out something that was very important to you. Something she wanted to tell you. But she didn't get to."

***

In my photograph, Flora's face no longer shone. It was heavy and serious. Maybe it was my gloomy mood that changed her facial features and appearance. I felt guilty. Shame. What kind of person had I become? Had I forgotten how happy Flora and I had once been? How fond we'd been of each other ... I'd betrayed her. I had opened Tilda's book before she was dead, even though she had expressly told me not to. I was to blame for her death ...

I felt time and space loosen my thoughts. I got up quickly, walked over to Flora's picture, took it in my hands, and clenched it to my chest. I sobbed. Tears rolled down my face and dripped onto the back of the

198

picture. I pressed the photograph tighter against my body, against each and every cell in my body.

The guilt was accompanied by compassion, and I heard myself say, "Forgive me, Flora." The sentence flew out of my mouth as if pushed out by something heartfelt inside me. "Forgive me. I've failed you ..." At that same moment, the picture fell to the floor. Terror-stricken I looked down to see if it was broken. It wasn't.

I hesitated for a moment with a feeling of gratitude.

As if thrown into another dimension with another gravity, I forgot my pain. Or it had disappeared of its own accord.

I hung the picture up. Flora's face lit up again.

25
THE BOOK

Chaos. On the street, in the air, in people's eyes. Even in the stars looking down at us from their fixed observation posts. Chaos.

The slightest movement, the slightest sound made me tremble. I paced back and forth … from room to room. From wall to wall … could hear my out-of-breath breathing. Feel my heart right up in my throat.

I went to the dresser in the living room and opened the top drawer. There it was.

Tilda's book. I started looking through it as if searching for an answer. What was it Flora wanted to tell me? Why had she let me keep the book? Tilda's wish was for Flora to inherit it. The faster I flipped through the pages, the more panicked I became.

I held my breath. Suddenly the book slipped out of my hands, lifted up, and floated under the ceiling. I stared in confusion at the book's black cover. Got dizzy. Heard the alarm clock ticking in the bedroom. The blood rose to my head. I sat down. Closed my eyes.

An answer appeared. An invisible hand wrote on a blackboard: *You must get away from here.*

***

The sun hadn't risen yet. I got out of bed, put on my bathrobe, went into the kitchen, drank a glass of cold herbal tea, went into the living room, and sat on the ottoman.

I heard steps. The door to the hall opened. A woman in her thirties entered the living room. She had shoulder-length brown hair, blue eyes, and spoke with an accent. "Excuse me for rushing in. I knocked, but when there was no answer, I opened the door. It wasn't locked."

She introduced herself. "My name is Amy and I know Augusto. I'm from Scotland and work for the WHO. We're leaving for Split tomorrow. There's a seat available. You're welcome to come along."

***

A Jeep pulled up in front of the house at four in the morning. The driver, a man in his forties, gave me a card and informed me it was my ID. I had to say I was working for the WHO when we were stopped at roadblocks.

We drove off. Amy drove in another car.

I was terrified. Didn't utter a word to the driver. He talked about the women in his life and complained that he couldn't use his education as a lawyer but had to be content with being a driver. He made a lot of money. He transported medical equipment from Split in Croatia to Bosnia-Herzegovina and distributed it to all ethnicities, including Serbs, he pointed out.

I heard the driver shout, "Wake up! We're here! We've arrived in Split!"

Usually I get cranky if someone wakes me, but this time it was the happiest way to wake up, and I felt I was still alive. To breathe in the scent of the Adriatic Sea. After hours and hours of dangerous driving. The driver said, "Go straight across the street. Amy lives in number three."

Split was a gathering place for several aid organizations that sent emergency aid to Bosnia-Herzegovina, and to a limited extent, organized evacuation convoys of refugees. Most refugees were accommodated in private houses and hotels, but a number of them traveled on to other countries.

Amy said I could stay in her apartment to start with. But later I had to manage myself.

26
SAFE
SPLIT, 1994

Amy served fried cod with balsamic, boiled potatoes, and steamed silver beets with olive oil and
garlic. But I couldn't eat. She told me my appetite would
probably return. "Just try a few bites to start."

It was hard to figure out what I should eat first—the
fish, the potatoes, or the silver beets. I just looked at
them.

In the afternoon, I took a potato and ate a bite. It
tasted weird.

It was twilight when we went out. I zigzagged from
one side of the street to the other. Hid in a stairwell,
then darted out with a startled look in my eyes.

Amy ran after me, stopped me, and said softly, "Don't
be afraid of snipers and grenades. You are safe here."

***

The phone rang. It was strange to hear that sound.
It was for me.

"From Santiago!" Amy said excitedly.

Alberto's voice sounded distant and unreal. He said they'd had a daughter. She could already smile, he said. I wanted to hold my new grandchild. He had talked with Alma who sent her greetings to everyone. She had gone to Denmark with her children after a long journey through Europe. They were being accommodated in a refugee center. Alma was going to write to me, so I shouldn't worry, he added. I said I'd call soon …

I went out onto the balcony. Lifted my head to the stars and looked at them as I smiled.

Amy learned there was a spare room in a hotel where refugees were staying, mostly women and children, and where the Red Cross had offices.

"Do you think it could be for you?" she asked.

It was easy to say yes without hesitation. I'd been staying with her for three months and was beginning to worry about my future.

The hotel lay on the outskirts of Split. The women had formed a society so they could help each other return to Bosnia and Herzegovina after the war.

27

The women
Split, 1995

Selma was an attractive woman in her thirties with long blonde hair and blue eyes. Her room was next to mine, and when she had a visit from a lover, I had to turn on the radio so as not to hear all the moans and screams penetrating through the wall.

She never talked about herself. All I knew was she came from Srebrenica and she had a husband who was a soldier in the Bosnian Army, but she didn't seem to care about him. She was just waiting to get a visa to go abroad.

Once her husband called to tell her he had been injured. Selma scolded him and said he could find comfort with another woman.

That same day she wrote to him:

I've found someone else. To hell with you, and all other soldiers, and your cursed war!

At five in the morning, I heard screams coming from Selma's room. Her lover was beating her, I thought.

When I knocked on her door, she opened it and showed me her swollen cheek. She had a toothache.

I went to Elvira, who was a dentist, woke her up, and asked if she could help Selma, but Elvira replied angrily, "Do you realize what time it is? If she can fuck anyone and everyone, she can handle a little toothache. I'm sure it doesn't hurt that much. I don't get a dime for my work and have to be available around the clock. I'm no humanitarian organization. I'm just an ordinary person who needs her sleep."

But Elvira got up, put on her tracksuit, and went to the clinic. Selma arrived just after her and sat in the dentist's chair. Elvira said, "So, beautiful, where does it hurt so much that you had to wake all the residents?"

Selma pointed to a molar and muttered, "It's killing me. Promise me you'll be gentle."

Elvira took a piece of gauze, dipped it in ether, placed it on the tooth, and asked, "How did you get the toothache? It's loose. Did your lover beat you?"

"No, he didn't. He's very sweet."

"You said that about the other men who did beat you. Where do you find those types? They treat you like a rag. But maybe they're good for something else."

Elvira examined the tooth and said resignedly, "I

have to pull it out. It's too loose. It can't be saved. And I have no anesthesia. It's going to hurt."

Selma screamed again and said she couldn't handle it, but Elvira said very loudly, "But you say the tooth hurts. What do you want more—for it to hurt all the time or just for a moment when I pull it?"

"Fine. Do it. But you have to tell me a joke."

"I promise," said Elvira. "Should I start now?"

Selma nodded, her eyes wide with fear.

Elvira hadn't even finished the joke when Selma started laughing. Her cheek, the swollen one, vibrated so much that her face was completely skewed.

The tooth was out, and Elvira said she was done.

I walked Selma up to her room. She opened the door, turned around, and with blood in her mouth muttered, "I'm pregnant. But I don't want the baby. The child's father is a Chetnik who raped me before I escaped. I'll have it removed when I get to Australia. I got a visa."

I asked Elvira if she thought she was being a little hard on Selma. She was surprised by the question and after a long pause answered, "Do you think so? Maybe I am. But why do I have to fight with her and the other women and their post-traumatic issues? I'm just a dentist, and I'm trying to do my best. They need a psychologist or a psychiatrist. You do too, by the way. I'm worried about your health. You hardly eat anything. We all need professional help. Talking about our problems is not enough. The war has left deep wounds. It's fine that aid organizations and the Croatian state are taking care of food, clothes, and accommodation. But we have to move on with our lives. Otherwise, we'll go to the dogs."

She asked if I wanted a cup of coffee. I said yes and we went into her room.

Elvira told me to sit down. She lit a cigarette and went out into the kitchen.

There was a sofa bed in the room, a dining table, and a couple of bookshelves. Family photos of all sizes, with and without frames, decorated an entire wall. I got up and went over to look. There were pictures of Elvira as a child, her siblings, father and mother, classmates … in the middle was a picture from her wedding. Elvira and her husband stood smiling in front of City Hall. In Dubrovnik. Strange, I thought. They stood in the same place where Pablo and I had been photographed when we got married. There was something about Elvira's wedding dress, it looked like the dress I had sewn when I was going to marry Niko and which I forgot to take from Niko's apartment when I left him. I looked at the groom ... my stomach lurched. I knew that smile. It *was* Niko! He had given her *my* wedding dress! She must have had the same measurements as me. I was horror-struck.

Suddenly Elvira was standing beside me. "He was handsome, my husband, wasn't he?"

"Was? Aren't you married anymore?"

"No. He was killed at Koševo Hospital in Sarajevo. He was a specialist and went to work every day while many of his colleagues left town."

"But you were married in Dubrovnik? I recognize City Hall. I got married there too. In the summer of 1964."

"Really! Niko and I got married that summer too. I met him at a bar. He came up to me and said something I will never forget ... that's how it started. We had only been together three times when he proposed. I must admit I was somewhat surprised. I liked him, but I didn't know if I was ready to get married. Still, I said yes. It was good I did. He was a loving man, full of understanding. We would have liked to have had children, but we didn't have any. The doctors couldn't find out why not, so I went to a fortune teller in Sarajevo ..." Elvira fell silent, and I asked, "Did you find out why?"

"Yes. She was right, and ..." Elvira didn't say more about the fortune teller but asked, "What about you? Have you ever been to a fortune teller?"

"Yes. Once. With a friend, and the fortune teller was partially right."

"Partially?"

"She said that my marriage would be unhappy. My husband and I had a good relationship, but I lost him. He was executed. The fortune teller left an impression on me. She had long white hair, big earrings, several rings on her fingers, three bracelets, and a few chains. Her eyes were blurry, her gaze distant. I would like to meet her again if she's still alive. Unfortunately my friend who knew her is dead. I think she kept a secret."

"Sounds strange. The fortune teller I visited had very long white hair, blurry eyes, and an unusual amount of jewelry. I know who it is ... Sara is related to her."

"Sara who?"

"The chairwoman of our refugee association. It's her *grandmother!*"

***

Sara was a beautiful young woman with pale skin

and long dark hair. She always spoke of her boyfriend, Jakob, and read his letters aloud.

I started looking for her. Someone thought she had gone to town to buy hair dye. Others said she had gone back to Sarajevo. I gave up and went up to my room.

Elvira appeared, out of breath, and told me not to look for Sara any longer.

They'd found her. I was happy, but Elvira burst into tears. I was confused and asked if something had happened. She held her breath and said, "They found her ... dead ... on the floor. Her heart could take no more. She was only thirty-six. She was the only bright spot in my life. I'm leaving now. Going far away."

I approached Elvira, wanting to hold her, but she went on her way.

Two months later, she got a visa, bought a one-way plane ticket, and traveled to Canada.

Split Municipality couldn't have refugees staying in the hotel any longer. We had to move in a few months. The hotel was to be renovated, much of the inventory had been destroyed.

The humanitarian aid was no longer enough, and

we still couldn't travel back to Sarajevo. The war wasn't over.

I asked Amy if I could stay at her place for a while. She said she had another refugee staying, but she could probably make room for me as well. She had to travel to Tuzla with new supplies anyway. There had been a massacre in Srebrenica.

I called Robert to find out what had happened to Kana and the kids, but I couldn't get through.

***

Amy had left and I moved into her apartment. The other refugee, a young woman, was rarely home. She said good morning, ate yogurt with half a pomegranate, left, and came back late at night after I had gone to bed.

Several weeks passed before I heard from Robert. He was still alive, he said on the phone, but he hadn't heard from Kana. He tried to get in touch with her and the children, but no one could say exactly what had happened to them. Some thought they'd managed to escape the massacre, said Robert, sounding on the verge of tears. "We should never have gone our separate ways. We quarreled over trifles. Now I see how stupid

I was, how much I misunderstood her. If I don't hear from them soon, I'm going to go there to find them. I don't care if it's dangerous. I haven't heard from Anton for several months either. The last time I spoke to him he was on leave. He said his unit was to move north. There has been fierce fighting there."

***

I went out into the kitchen. The woman I lived with was sitting eating her yogurt with half a pomegranate. She said good morning and smiled for the first time. Her name was Esmeralda, and she came from northwestern Bosnia, near the Croatian border. She asked if she could tell me something before she had to leave the next morning. It was important that someone knew what had happened. She could not keep it to herself any longer.

I didn't know what to say. I didn't know her, she didn't know me either, I had nothing to do with her. I didn't know if I could handle it. It was probably more talk of suffering and distress that she wanted to share with me, but I was dizzy from war and pain. I wanted to go on my way or shut myself in my room, lie down, and read a book.

But I said yes to hearing what she had to say.

She fetched a bottle of cognac and two glasses. Poured the amber liquid into the glasses and gave me one. She lit a cigarette and took a drag. Afterward, she drained the whole glass in one gulp. And one more.

In her asthmatic voice, Esmeralda began:

28

ESMERALDA

*I*n Bosanska Gradiška, where I come from, the war began in August 1991. Serbian soldiers entered the town and raised three fingers in the air, their sign of victory. A few days later, the first inhabitants were killed.

The paramilitary unit under the Serbian police, the "Scorpions," ordered mobilization and drove around in vans arresting people, beating them, and throwing them into trucks like sacks.

A resistance group pushed across the Sava River into the city and attacked the "Scorpions." In revenge, the Chetniks blew up cafés and mosques. Many were killed. Their hands were tied behind their backs, their heads chopped off.

The war hadn't yet begun in Sarajevo, but thousands of people had been killed and people deprived of their homes and land in Bosanska Gradiška and other towns in northern Bosnia. In the capital, the government did nothing.

One day in May 1992, I wanted to show a refugee going back to Croatia the way to the Sava Bridge. But we

*were arrested and imprisoned, even though we had the
necessary papers.*

*I was interrogated. An officer demanded information
about Croats, whom I didn't know at all. He beat me up.
Stubbed out cigarettes on my feet and thighs, my breasts,
my stomach …*

*Several men held my arms, my legs, and my head. A
few others raped me.*

*When I came to, I was covered in blood and semen. I
had bruises and scratches and cuts all over my body. I was
raped again and—*

Esmeralda didn't manage to finish the sentence
because I yelled for her to stop. "I can't listen to it
anymore! I've had enough. Do you think you can
just tell stories like that and assume they won't affect
people? You don't know me. I want nothing to do with
it. I will decide for myself! I will not be affected by your
fate."

She looked at me in shock, got up, and went into her
room. The next morning, she was gone.

***

The storm had destroyed the balcony in Amy's

apartment. Rubble and dust lay everywhere, the potted plants had been knocked over and smashed. Fragments of Christmas decorations lay on the street along with branches and plastic bags.

The phone rang. The connection hadn't been broken by the wind, I thought. I rushed to answer it. A distant voice at the other end of the receiver said, "Masha, my love, how nice it is to hear your voice. How are you feeling?"

I sat down, moving the receiver to the other hand. It was Anton. I didn't know if I was dreaming.

He had come back from the front. He was never to be a soldier again, he had cast aside his uniform. He said excitedly, "The war is over. There is peace now. Come home!"

29

Return
Sarajevo, 1996

Impatiently, with shaking hands, Anton began to undress me. The smell of cigarettes from his mouth nauseated me, and I said I couldn't sleep with him. "I need more time. I have to get used to you again."

But Anton insisted. "It's been so long. I want you. I want to feel you, your movements, I want to kiss you all over."

I lay down on the bed, even though I didn't want to. I seemed to be enchanted by his words.

Anton touched my breasts. He licked my ears, my neck, and asked me to touch his wounded leg. "Your hands have magical powers. My leg will be healed," he moaned with deep breaths.

I let him push into me. He came quickly and I felt his happiness. Seeing him satisfied I felt like pleasing him against my will. He said he missed me and began talking about our future.

I didn't listen to Anton anymore but thought about Vanja instead. She had turned up earlier in the evening to say she had been inspired by a new radio program for women. It gave her courage and strength. She believed women would soon take power from men. "Those war-crazed men need to understand their days are numbered. A new era is on its way across the globe. Long live the Feminine Age!" shouted Vanja.

I smiled. Anton's eyes lit up. He sat down, lit a cigarette, and said, "That was just what I needed. After such a long time. Your mind seemed to be somewhere else. Is something wrong?"

I didn't know what I wanted to say, but I replied anyway. "I haven't heard from you in almost two years, and you act like nothing has happened. So much has happened. I have changed."

He looked at me in surprise and explained that I hadn't heard from him because he was fighting. He emphasized the last word. "I was in trenches, in mud, in bunkers most of the time. I was close to death at every moment. Hungry and thirsty. And anxious. We fought in the mountains, far away from civilization. Face to face with the enemy. I'm not the same person as I was before either, but we have to get used to each other again. That takes time."

"I know well that it takes time. But I can't. You were away when I needed you most. I know it's hard for you.

You were wounded, your leg still hurts—"

Anton interrupted me. "And my friends and comrades were killed, have disappeared, fled. My father was executed. But what is unbearable is that those who didn't fight have seized power. They don't care that the rest of us sacrificed our lives. The only thing they're interested in is lining their pockets and getting big cars and apartments. Instead of rebuilding our homes, they're rebuilding mosques—even building new ones that don't even fit in with Bosnian style and tradition and churches that resemble concrete blocks. They abuse our suffering."

"Abuse how?"

"You only just came back. I've been in the country the whole time. But I didn't fight for religion to be used politically, for us to be divided by faith. I fought against the fascists, the nationalists, those keeping our city under siege for three and a half years. People can believe what they want. It's a private matter. And religion can't be decisive for whether I can get disability pension. I am entitled to it by law. Still, I get only a pittance that I can't live on. They haven't offered me a job either."

"I understand you're disappointed. And everything is destroyed. Many people lost their lives, families have been torn apart. Thousands of refugees have arrived, people with different cultures. But I'm home. And I want to help rebuild the city."

"Good luck with that. I've tried but was mostly prevented from doing so. All they're doing is waiting on money from abroad. What do you actually want, Masha?"

"Find work. Maybe I can get a job in a kindergarten for orphaned children. Two women who were refugees in Split and who have now returned are looking into the possibilities. Maybe a humanitarian organization can fund most of it. But I don't think we can live together anymore. We have to find out which of us will stay in the apartment."

"You talk as if it's easy to find somewhere to live. Where will you live if you're the one who has to move?"

"Maybe I'll move in with Robert or Augusto. I'll figure it out."

"So you want a divorce? What do you think is best for us? How can you decide for both of us?"

"It's not something I planned. The two years the war separated us ripped our good years to shreds. We've become distant with each other. Do you think it's fun to be together when I can't stand sleeping with you? I'm sorry. I really am. People blame me because I fled during the war, but I did it to save my life … and no one will give me a guilty conscience. Just because they think they went through the worst of it. Perhaps, deep down they chose the role of martyr …"

"You say we've become distant. I haven't grown distant from you. You're no stranger to me."

"But you can't force me to love you again. I'm not the same woman as when we lived together."

"So who are you?"

"I don't know. I have to figure it out. It's hard to explain. Right now I'm trying to understand the connection between some mysterious events that have happened. It's like I'm living two simultaneous lives. One life where I try to survive and do everyday things and another life that isn't physical but takes place in a parallel world where I have to clear up some mysteries to find meaning, to find myself."

I woke terror-stricken from a dream. It was dark. My clothes were drenched in sweat. I lay down again and tried to remember the dream:

Anton's horses were sniffing each other's muzzles, whinnying. I felt their warmth. Their stomachs jerked, they jumped, galloped aimlessly. When they saw me, they started kicking me in the chest, in the lungs. Their blood boiled and I collapsed. My back, kidneys, and ankles were crushed under their legs. They stomped on my neck and head. I tried to cry out for help but couldn't.

I turned into a bloody mass that hardened into a lump of lead that bore into the straw floor. The stable wall crumbled and crashed down. The ground was wet with spring.

The blood gushed from me stronger and stronger. A sour, corrosive stench spread in the stable. My lips parted. A sound came from my crushed chest. I whispered Anton's name, yearning for his touch. My voice rang through his parents' cornfields. But no one came. Only a breeze cooled my torn flesh.

***

Sarajevo's morning light crept in through the greasy curtains. I raised my head and sat up. The smell of the quinces on top of the wardrobe reminded me of a remote, happy time.

I lay down again. Sweat dripped from my forehead, chest, and armpits. I lay with my back glued to the bed. Noticed a bullet hole in the wall opposite. For a moment the hole seemed to disappear, and the wall turned into a screen. I saw Anton say goodbye. He limped and spoke in a subdued but piercing voice. "I'm going to miss you."

Anton tried to hold me, but he stumbled, his legs couldn't support him. His eyes looked through mine, revealing regret. I looked down. My lips moistened his cheek, and I heard myself say, "Take care of yourself."

The taxi honked impatiently. Anton hurried to limp down the stairs, through the gate, into the car.

He disappeared from my field of vision behind the curtain. Away from the streets of Sarajevo.

He only left yesterday, but it felt like an eternity ago.

The bedroom lighting cast a secretive glow on the wall. There was a picture from mine and Anton's wedding. My head was heavy and foggy. I stayed in bed, lost in despair.

***

There was a letter on the floor in the hall. The mailman wouldn't ring the doorbell. Maybe to avoid having to say hello, I thought. I picked up the letter. On the back was the sender's name and address.

Alma!

The sun licked my cheeks. I tore open the envelope and began to read:

225

30

ALMA

COPENHAGEN, SEPTEMBER 11, 1996

Dear Mother,

I'm so glad you've come home. How are you? It's been so long. I don't know where to start.

Our journey to Denmark took a long time. We had to change buses three times. Finally we boarded a Polish ferry in Świnoujście. We woke up when the ferry arrived in the port of Copenhagen.

We were met by a police officer and an interpreter. The interpreter examined our documents and decided who was to be rejected.

We were driven to a refugee camp surrounded by barbed wire fences. Hundreds of people were crammed together in a large tent, and I was gripped by the same panic and anxiety as during the war. An interpreter called us in, one by one, to be interrogated.

At two o'clock in the morning, we were driven to a refugee center in Copenhagen.

For a long time, we could neither learn Danish nor work. But I have started to learn the language now, and the children have been allowed to go to kindergarten.

There are rumors that Bosnians will soon get residence and work permits.

Veronika has become quite shy. Igor still thinks there is a war. He draws machine guns and bombs, and when he hears an airplane, he screams and asks for his father. One of the kindergarten teachers thinks I should take him to a psychologist. Her name is Britta, and she has invited the children and me to her mother's house. Britta is not allowed to see the kindergarten's children in private, but she is making an exception for us, she says. She is the only Dane we know.

Kosta is alive. He has come to Denmark! He sought me out a few days ago while the children were in kindergarten. I was shocked. His eyes were red and his hair gray. He was drunk and told me what he and his militia comrades had done during the war. Kosta was part of the attack on Lipik! They destroyed Anton's stud with cannons and grenades. A fire broke out, and many of the horses caught fire and suffocated from the smoke. The horses that escaped were *shot down and the militia built barricades from the dead horses.*

Crying, I said I didn't want to hear about it anymore, but he refused to leave before he'd told me the whole story.

To think that Grandad died from his shot! I don't know what has happened to him. It's like he's possessed.

He said he was in Denmark to get the children. But I don't want him to see them when he's drunk. I'm afraid of what he might do. How can I forgive him? I hope that one day he will repent and realize he has been tricked and misled.

Looking forward to hearing from you. Write about everything and everyone.

Lots of love,
Your Alma

31

ALIVE
SARAJEVO, SEPTEMBER 1996

A gust of wind from the open window brought papers and lint into the living room. Half-darkened walls slipped away. A pain had settled in my stomach. A figure followed my breathing. A voice rang out as if it came from another world. It sounded like Kana's voice. Maybe Robert had heard from her. Had she managed to escape from Srebrenica?

The mailman rang. I opened the door. He had a registered letter for me. I had to sign a form, and before I could say anything he was already on his way down the stairs.

When I opened the envelope there were two other envelopes inside. A small, thin one with a letter in it and a thick one that was closed. Alma had written that it shouldn't be opened before I had read the letter in the small envelope:

Copenhagen, September 22, 1996

Dear Mother,

I have something important to tell you. Kana, Uncle Robert's ex-wife, is alive. She is in Denmark!

I found out recently when I visited an acquaintance in the hospital. Kana is very thin, pale, and has no hair. She has lung cancer and has had radiation treatment and chemotherapy. Now the cancer has spread, and she is in excruciating pain.

But it is not her illness that troubles her. It's her guilty conscience. She believes she survived at the cost of her son.

She says I am to ask you to forgive her for pestering you with phone calls and for forewarning that you and Dad would divorce. Back then, she was possessed by an evil force that destroyed her marriage too. And she blindly believed something that a fortune teller had told her. She was unable to distinguish between fact and fiction. She mentioned she knew Flora. They had been at the fortune teller's together, and the woman had performed some rituals to free Flora from a curse.

Kana believes the suffering she experienced during the war was due partly to the evil force that had taken power over her life. But I don't agree. I believe the war was part of a plan to seize territory and commit genocide. Kana admits that sounds logical, but she still insists that certain people became victims. People who are already trapped in a vicious circle easily fall into the hands of the executioners who are also possessed by a destructive energy, just to a much greater extent.

It pains Kana that she doesn't know much about the fortune teller. She needs to gather some threads to learn exactly what the woman told her, what she knew, and why Flora and she spoke in codes. According to Kana, there are several loose ends, and she would like to find a connection.

She gave me a notebook and asked me to read aloud from it. She said, "When you've done that, I can go in peace."

I've just read it. I've enclosed a copy for you. Give it to Uncle Robert too.

Hugs and kisses,
Alma

Another story about the ravages of war was my first thought once I finished Alma's letter. I had decided not to focus on the war but on the here and now instead. But I was curious and eager to know Kana's story.

Kana wrote:

32

KANA
SREBRENICA, APRIL 1992

I was at the hairdresser's when Arkan's and Šešelj's militias, both men and women, started shooting in the streets. We ran into the basement along with a woman with strips of silver foil and dye in her hair, a man who was half-barbered, a girl with long wet hair, and myself with a women's magazine in my hand.

I hid behind a couch in a shed in the basement while the others sat on rag rugs in a large room directly opposite the shed. I heard footsteps upstairs in the salon, things falling, shots fired from automatic pistols, mirrors breaking. The militia combatants talked loudly and laughed. I heard quick steps down the stairs to the basement. I saw three black-clad men and a woman storm into the basement. The woman had a bottle of shampoo in each trouser pocket, a tin of hairspray in her left hand, and a rifle in her right. The men grabbed the man with the half haircut and slit his throat. The militia woman beat the woman with the strips of foil and dye in her hair until she died. The black-clad man pulled his pants down and threw himself at the young girl with long wet hair. The girl screamed. She was raped and shot.

Srebrenica, 1993

General Morillon declared Srebrenica a UN-protected zone!

When winter came, a humanitarian convoy escaped through the obstacles. Thousands of starving people lined the roads and waved at the soldiers.

A man asked, "What kind of flags do they have on the vehicles?"

A woman replied, "Danish. There are rumors they are going to evacuate people. But it's not certain there'll be room for everyone."

In the morning, my sister Selma and I hurried to a truck in the neighboring street. The truck was already overcrowded. People hung over the sides. We tried to jump up but were pushed away.

My children, Mina and Alan, managed to escape to Tuzla with my mother. Selma's husband signed up for a unit in the Bosnian Army. Selma and I moved into a garage with a group of other refugees.

We sat and slept on quilts, blankets, and clothes. When we heard shots, we huddled together and stopped talking. Icicles hung from the ceiling.

Srebrenica, 1994

A military corps from Serbia advanced closer and closer on the town.

Several men who lived with us in the garage joined a Bosnian brigade.

They raided Serbian targets for food and ammunition.

Srebrenica, 1995

Serbian forces led by Mladić pushed one mile into the protected zone.

Selma and I still lived in the garage. At the beginning of July, a three-year-old boy died of hunger. We had no more jars of preserves or powdered milk.

There was panic in the streets. Large groups spontaneously began to head toward the UN base in the village of Potočari. Selma said she was going too. "I'll die if I stay in this cursed city. I'm going to seek protection from the Dutch soldiers. Maybe they can drive me to the Bosnian Army."

She asked if I wanted to come along, but I had my doubts. "When General Morillon declared Srebrenica a protected zone, I still had hope. Now I don't know who or what to trust?"

Selma was wearing her turquoise dress when we said goodbye. She started walking toward Potočari. Her long blonde hair fluttered in the wind, and her blue eyes reflected the blue sky.

I walked with half a dozen women, children, and men desperate to find their way to the liberated area.

On July 11, we reached the village of Jaglić where several hundred people had gathered. A woman came running to say the military base in Potočari had fallen. The base had been surrounded by Mladić's artillery and tanks, and the Dutch soldiers hadn't resisted. The Chetniks had disarmed the soldiers and put barbed wire around the base."

Our group joined a column where an armed man ordered, "No talking. Walk! We don't have much time."

It was eighty-six degrees Fahrenheit. We trudged off. After half an hour the Chetniks started shooting. The man in front of me fell over, hit by a shell. I ran back a little, we ran in separate directions. I rushed behind a rock and hid.

The attacks stopped. I looked around. Couldn't see the two men I was with. I started looking for them. Dead lay everywhere. A wounded man wailed. A woman called for her son. When she found him dead, she fainted. A little girl sat on a rock. She got up and called for her mother. An elderly woman comforted her. Two women provided first aid, cleaned wounds, and bound them with bandages and remnants of clothing.

We paused for a moment. My feet hurt. When I went to sit down, the order was given to leave. I was knocked over and carried away by the crowd.

The armed men walked at the front and back of the column, the wounded and healthy between them. The badly wounded lay on stretchers of branches and laths.

The column was split up into several smaller groups. I still had pain in my feet, but I thought about my children and my mother.

The shootings continued. Several were killed.

A woman tugged my arm and whispered, "We've reached the village of Buljim."

The night was wet with rain. We walked silently through a forest. Suddenly someone collapsed. The woman and I stopped for a moment. Several people collapsed. I sensed her bewildered eyes. She gestured as if to ask what was going on. Before she could finish waving her arms, she collapsed. When I felt her bleeding, it dawned on me what was happening. The Chetniks had penetrated the column and were killing without noise, with knives. People crumpled without a single shot being fired. We were caught in an ambush. I started running, tripping over corpses. My legs could still carry me.

The armed men started shooting at the Chetniks. My body swayed, but a man grabbed me by the arm and said, "Keep going. Don't give up. We will soon be free."

The attacks continued. We couldn't go the same way, so changed route.

We walked for ages. The man who spoke of freedom collapsed. Soon more followed. A rest was ordered.

An old woman gave me a few dandelion leaves and a black slug. She sprinkled salt on it before I stuffed them in my mouth.

I squatted down with the others. The earth was parched by the July sun. The cracks crumbled under my blistered feet.

Someone yelled, "A puddle!"

People threw themselves at the puddle.

Someone else shouted, "Look, there's a river! We're saved."

In only a few seconds the river was transformed into an orgy of cheers. A girl remarked the water tasted sweet.

In the midst of the cheering, we heard an explosion. One of the armed men shouted, "Get away, get away! There are mines!"

The blood from torn bodies flowed into the river, staining the water. The woman who had given me salt lost her leg. The two women who had provided first aid ran to the injured. A little boy called for his mother. The group leader gave the order, "We leave in ten minutes. Walk in single file."

There was only one column left.

At night we sat in silence under rocks and bushes. Weren't allowed to cough, clear our throats, sneeze. The Chetniks were only about 150 feet away. I cowered.

I dozed off under a rock. Woken at dawn by a bang. The ground shook. A grenade had hit a rock. A man next to me had his leg ripped into pieces that flew through the air.

I lay on the ground and could see a glimpse of the Jadar river, and a cloud of dust and fire.

It rained all day. The river was cloudy with mud. A woman took my hand. We waded across the river. The water was up to our chests. We held on to each other so as not to be sucked away by the current, which pulled us like a hungry sea serpent. I bent down to drink water. But the woman exclaimed, "Don't drink it. It could kill you."

Several people began to wail. Others screamed. Some became delirious. I asked the woman what was happening. She explained the water they were drinking had been poisoned. People had fever fits. A man stared with eyes full of fear and began to shoot wildly all around him. A gunman blew himself up with a hand grenade. Another shot himself in the head but missed. He asked a woman to end his life. She burst into tears.

I thought of Selma. I thought about where she was, whether she was alive.

I missed my children. And my mother. They were waiting for me in the liberated area.

At the village of Kamenica, our column was attacked with grenades and anti-aircraft fire. Suddenly a girl said, "Look, the bridge to Kamenica."

Several people ran over the bridge but were met with artillery. A few of them reached the other side. The girl and I hid behind a hedge.

Shells rained down on us from seven o'clock in the

evening until half past three in the morning. I felt the dead and wounded fall around me. A foul odor spread.

A dense fog settled over us. The Chetniks had advanced. One of them shouted that we were defeated and we should surrender.

The girl and I surrendered along with half a dozen others.

They took us to the sports field in the village of Kravica. They separated men from women. The women were allowed to go.

We walked and walked. Many, many hours later we reached the liberated area.

Old men, women, and children waited, looking with expectant eyes. They asked if we had seen their relatives.

My mother came running. We threw ourselves into each other's arms. We held each other for a long time, tasting each other's tears. Her face had become pale, her wrinkles coarse and deep.

A bus took us to the refugee camp at Tuzla airport. When we arrived, Alan ran to meet me. I touched his hands, arms, neck. Kissed his cheeks. Mina and I spotted each other. We burst into tears.

The sun was scorching. It was Alan's birthday. Mina was playing with a friend. My mother and I sat on the grass in front of our barracks, drinking coffee. Alan sat with us for a while but began to feel bored and went to the playground.

My mother said she hadn't heard from Selma. She didn't manage to say more as she was interrupted by a loud explosion. We huddled together and hid our faces in our arms.

A moment after we jumped up at the same time and ran toward the playground.

Alan lay with a ball in his hand. Dead. I stood staring at him without moving. Felt a pressure in my lungs. It was as if it wasn't me who was looking at his torn body. Like it wasn't my son.

My mother took care of Mina, but it was hard for her. She had pain in her stomach.

When my mother heard that the mayor of Tuzla, Selma's former boyfriend, was to pay an official visit to Sarajevo, Mina was allowed to join his military escort. My mother moved in with a cousin on the outskirts of Tuzla.

I still hadn't heard from Selma after our parting in Srebrenica. I looked for her in the refugee camp, but no one had seen her.

One day I bumped into a woman at one of the barracks and we got to chatting. It turned out she had been with Selma at the UN military base in Potočari. Suddenly she got pains in her legs and sat down on a bench. I sat down next to her. She stank of cigarettes. Her yellow fingers trembled. She took a deep breath and said, "We were to be driven from the base. When we reached the buses, Serbian soldiers separated boys and men between fifteen and sixty from the rest of us. Many were executed in the fields, on the sports ground, in the valley. Corpses lay on corpses. Sons, husbands, brothers, uncles.

A group of women were ordered to board a bus. They were raped and shot. Three soldiers took out the bodies and threw them at our feet. We, the group of women who remained, were ordered onto the bus. Selma and I sat next to each other. The engine was started and the bus drove. It stopped after half an hour.

A soldier with a machine gun in his hand shouted for us to get out.

We got out. The soldier went from one woman to another. Picked out the six youngest and prettiest. Selma was one of them. He assessed them quickly and said they were good for breeding. He and another soldier led the women toward the forest. A third kept watch at the bus. Something moved behind a bush. The soldier approached it cautiously. At that moment, I ran across the road toward the edge of the forest. I ran faster and faster. I managed to escape. I don't know if Selma managed to escape or what happened to her."

33
The Stars
Sarajevo, September 1996

Beads of sweat ran between my breasts and down my stomach and legs. I opened my eyes. My hair was wet and sticky. The clammy September night crept in through the open window. I jumped out of bed, grabbed my bathrobe from the chair next to it, flung it around my naked body, hastened to the window, and turned my sweaty face to the stars. Their presence penetrated my body. It soothed, relaxed. I could control the thoughts that had flown through my head a moment ago. Compassion and love for Kana and Selma filled me. Crimes and ravages were part of a distant memory. Not to be forgotten.

34
THE WEDDING PHOTO
SARAJEVO, OCTOBER 12, 1996

Out in the yard a black cat wandered by. The air was cold. I closed the window and sat on the bed. An amber star peered down through the window. An uneasiness settled over the bedroom. I stood up and took Anton and my wedding photo from the wall. Went to the closet and opened a cardboard box. As I was about to put the picture in it, I spotted a piece of paper. I unfolded it and recognized Anton's handwriting:

Dear Olga, I have to go to the front. Don't know when we'll see each other again. But when I come back, I will feel your scent with my longing and my pain. Anton.

My stomach lurched. A mistress who had lived in our home! While I was in Split. How long had it been going on?

I went over to the bed. Collapsed onto it. Sweat trickled down my back, sticking to my bathrobe. I got up again. Instructions for homemade candles lay on the floor. I folded it up and threw it in the trash.

I took Niko's button from the pocket of the robe and caressed it.

Went back to the bed again and lay down. Went through the last hour, like that time when I saw a grenade explode for the first time and thought the final seconds of my life had arrived. The grenade's silver-blue and light-purple colors shot through the roofs, resembling a flower exploding into a myriad of smaller flowers in similar shades. As if the grenade's intense light had come from the sky. To show the way? Was the war a cleansing process to make way for a new, better time?

In the morning I tried to write to Alma but tore letter after letter to pieces. In the evening I was still in doubt about whether the final version was right. But the next morning I sent the letter:

35
NEW LIFE
SARAJEVO, OCTOBER 13, 1996

Dear Alma,

I'm so sorry that Kana is seriously ill and for what she endured during the war. Please give her my love and tell her that I don't give those phone calls or her warning a second thought. I have long since forgiven her. What I do find mysterious is only discovering now that she knew Flora.

Something amazing happened. Kana's sister Selma is alive! I lived near Selma in Split. I didn't know she was Kana's sister. She never visited us in Sarajevo. I clearly remember Selma's long blonde hair and her blue eyes. She wasn't terribly happy with her husband, who was a soldier, and she talked about a sister without naming her. I went to the dentist with her once. Before I returned to Sarajevo, she got a refugee visa and traveled to Australia. Perhaps she doesn't want to be in contact with the family and husband. Perhaps because she was expecting a child whose father was a Serbian soldier who raped her. Don't tell Kana that, she'll just get upset. But you are welcome to tell her everything else.

Robert tried to take his life when he heard that Alan had been killed. He thinks about Kana a lot, believes it's all his fault. If they hadn't divorced, she would never have returned to Srebrenica, he says. He would like to visit her, but he can't afford to unless he gets a job. He lives only for Mina's sake, he says. Mina misses her mother and wants to see her. Can you find out whether she can visit Kana in Denmark?

Augusto has finished his studies, but he hasn't yet found a job. He doesn't go out that much. I think he's still thinking about Minka.

Anton has gone to Lipik. I'm sorry, but I can't live with him any longer. I feel we have nothing in common anymore.

Sarajevo is gravely destroyed. Only six houses on our street haven't been demolished, there is no asphalt, only bunkers. Many people have been killed or fled. In our building, there's only Vanja, her husband, and me left of the old residents. Two new families moved in without permission.

Some new cafés have opened, and at the Markale market, you can now buy strawberries from the Serbian part of the country. A year after the massacre.

I got a job in a kindergarten—life has changed. I don't worry about trifles anymore. I can feel a new, strong energy. But when I'm not myself, I doubt whether I genuinely have changed or if it's all a delusion. Even though I didn't immediately believe what the fortune teller said, and even though I wasn't superstitious, it still affected me so much that I now find myself struggling with something I can't explain and for which I have to find a solution and free myself from.

I believe, like your father, that you can change your fate. He believed that our meeting was no coincidence. But he wouldn't let destiny rule his life. He had a strong will.

I miss Veronika and Igor. Take care of them and yourself. Hugs and kisses to all.

Love, Mom

36

Our own apartment
Copenhagen, October 26, 1996

Dear Mom,

I'm sorry that you and Anton aren't together anymore. I know things have been hard for you. But you're a survivor. Anton, though, gets quickly frustrated and gives up. You have to help him. He stood by your side while you built your career. And he has been a good father to us.

Kana is still very weak. She doesn't eat much. She is happy that Selma is alive. I'm convinced that it was the same Selma you lived with in Split. Kana has asked me to try to track down Selma in Australia.

Britta, the teacher at the kindergarten, wants to investigate whether Mina can come to Denmark to visit her mother.

I've started to look for work as a nurse and hope that I will get something soon. I can speak Danish now.

Britta's parents have given us permission to live in an apartment in their house. We have a kitchen, a bathroom, and two bedrooms.

We look after their dogs once in a while. Two Newfoundlands. I've learned a lot about dogs. I'd like to tell you something funny. When a dog is to be paired with another dog, it's best they have different attributes. But they can't be completely different. Otherwise, you don't know what will come out of it. The same applies to people, says Britta's mom. If the partners are too different, living together becomes hard.

I am divorcing Kosta. I haven't heard from him in a long time.

Lots of love,
Alma
Big hug from the kids!

37
REFLECTION
SARAJEVO, NOVEMBER 1996

To forgive others. To forgive yourself. To reconcile with yourself. With others.

I just can't reconcile with Anton right now. I have to follow my inner voice. No one else should decide how I am to live my life. Not even Alma.

***

Things were going better with Robert's daughter, Mina. She had stopped playing truant from school. And was happy she would be allowed to visit her mother in Denmark. Robert had to find out how to get money for the trip. When he came by, he said, "And you're feeling better too, I can see. New hair, makeup, perfume. Just like in the good old days."

"Yes. Except that Vanja knocks now and then. She showed up recently at two o'clock in the morning. I asked if she could come later in the morning, but she wouldn't listen. She sat down in the armchair and began to tell me about someone who had been in America thirty or forty years ago and who had long since died. I asked myself what use all this was to me and why she didn't consider me in her story. She said she'd taken a sleeping pill and didn't expect to be able to talk for long. But more than an hour passed, and I told her to go home and sleep. Then she left without saying goodbye.

"The next morning she called, scolded me, and explained she couldn't sleep because of me and it was me who had let her talk for so long. By then I'd had enough. I said she was going too far and I was not responsible for what she did. Then she said I could just have said good night. I reproached her. I'm fine with arguing instead of keeping things to myself and pretending everything is okay."

Robert considered me strangely. "And this is coming from you, you who pretended that you and Pablo had no problems. As though you were the happiest couple in the whole world."

"We were."

"But he cheated on you. You've hidden it well."

"How do you know that?"

"From Anton."

"Anton? I never discussed it with Anton."

"No, but you did with Flora."

"And?"

"She told Anton, and he told me."

"Flora told Anton? I don't believe it."

"Does it matter who told who? The point is you pretend everything is in perfect order. When I think about how Kana was jealous of your life. I wish she'd lived her own life, our life, and hadn't obsessed over you and Pablo breaking up. It occupied her so much that she became melancholy. And I couldn't do anything about it."

"Now I understand why she called Santiago and asked how things were going. But Pablo and I *were* happy."

"It depends on what you mean by happy. You see what you want to see."

"I was happy. Is it so hard to accept? Just because you had a bad marriage, doesn't mean you need to pass it on to others."

"You pretended you wanted to follow love, but in reality, you wanted to run away from home, and Niko was an obvious victim."

"That's not true!. You're living in your own world. Fine. But let's stop speaking ill about Kana. She is an honest person. And I have forgiven her for what she did."

Robert slammed the door and left.

***

I went to the phone and found the number of Sara's boyfriend, Jakob. Her sudden death in Split tormented me, and I couldn't stop thinking about what she actually died of back when she had been chair of the refugee association. Why she had to die so young was still a mystery to me. Just when I'd gotten the chance to ask her about her grandmother, the mysterious fortune teller, and why Flora was behaving strangely when I met her at the fortune teller's. Why had Kana and Flora sought her out together? And what was the code in Flora's poem? The unsolved questions rummaged around in my head. Maybe Jakob knew something. Maybe he could help me solve the mystery.

***

The sun shone on Jakob's handsome face as we sat drinking beer in a café. There was a glimmer of gloom in his eyes.

He and Sara had met at the Jewish humanitarian organization, *La Benevolencija*, where they distributed medicine. But after Sara was close to being killed, he arranged for her to escape the city in the organization's car. He enlisted in the Bosnian Army so as not to be watching passively when the next victim of the war was taken.

Now unemployed, he was looking for a job, anything. He would perish if he didn't find something to occupy himself.

I told him why I'd wanted to meet with Sara that fateful day when we lived in Split where she died unexpectedly.

He missed her a lot, he said. And he had heard about Tilda, who knew Sara's grandmother. "Both of them could see through our world and into the future. I was fascinated."

I told him I had once been at Sara's grandmother's.

"She guessed something about my life, even though I don't believe in that sort of thing. But I've had some mysterious experiences … it's difficult to explain."

I didn't share my experiences but changed the subject and said I could ask the kindergarten where I worked if they needed an extra worker. That made Jakob happy. "Please do. I like children. Sara and I talked about having some."

He looked down and took a drag of his cigarette.

I asked him to do me a favor. "If you come across

anything written by Sara's grandmother or Tilda in your apartment—a book, a piece of paper mentioning a ritual or something similar—will you give it to me?"

He nodded.

***

I look in the mirror. My eyes are red, tormented. My eyelids swelled. The wrinkles have found permanent places on my face. Blood courses through my body.

I have to escape. From what is plaguing me. Quickly and without doubt. Like the time I fled with Niko to Dubrovnik, away from the feeling that something terrible was going to happen to Sarajevo. Now I know the "the cruel thing" coming was the war. It has changed everything I believed in and fought for.

I have to escape. To a place inside me. A new mind.

38
DECISION
COPENHAGEN, NOVEMBER 21, 1996

Dear Mom,

I've decided to stay in Denmark. At first, I doubted whether I should. But now I can't imagine another life. Maybe because you feel safer here than elsewhere. I know there is no such thing as a perfect country. But I have realized that this is where I thrive most. And the children are doing well.

Arne, Britta's brother, who works in a computer company, taught the children computer games. He has also invited me to an exhibition. I'm looking forward to it, I feel like a whole person again.

Kana is getting thinner and thinner. But she is at peace. She is convinced that Robert will succeed in finding the money for Mina's trip and that she will get to see her while she is still alive.

I received a letter from Anton. He's not coming back to Sarajevo. He is going to stay in his hometown and is planning to open a riding school with Lipizzaner horses.

Why do we always dream of perfect relationships and families? Something that doesn't exist.

Lots of love,
Your Alma

39
TILDA'S BOOK
SARAJEVO, DECEMBER 6, 1996

As if in a trance, I watched the experiences from the war pass by. Their misery dissolved in the haze of heat, irrigating my brain with renewed strength. A dream surged forth from the beyond:

I rode a stallion. A breeze tickled my nostrils. A mare appeared and the horses nuzzled each other's muzzles and drowned in a kiss.

I didn't call for Anton. I didn't call for Pablo.

"The book!" I heard myself say out loud. I went to the display cabinet in the living room. Grabbed Tilda's book and held it tightly in my hands. Its black leather binding shone in the morning light. How could I forget I could now read it?

I opened it. The title page read: *The Secret Book* by Tilda Gaon.

On the next page, Tilda had written: "When you have experienced that everything in life is bound together for eternity, you have understood the beauty of life."

Carefully I began to turn the yellowed and worn pages on which she had written in neat, clear handwriting. The book was divided into chapters with titles such as "Folk Medicine," which contained cures for diseases, recipes for Jewish holidays, prayers, and instructions for reading the Torah on the individual days of the week, and "Old Sephardic Songs." One chapter was called, "Nature." I started reading:

God gave us Nature. It is pure and has its own laws. If you don't respect them, Nature can be destroyed. When it is destroyed, it becomes wounded and then it kills.

Another chapter was entitled: "Spiritual Life and Wisdom":

A world exists outside of space and time, our world has a connection to infinity. I believe that a supreme being stands behind Nature and everything. That the

Universe is not governed by chance. That everything is energy, vibration.

Everything is made of light in accordance with the law of eternal mathematics. God is the soul of light … When a human soul calls forth a thought, the sign of the thought is written in the light. Beware of gloomy thoughts and melancholy, anger, and feelings of revenge. Cleanse your soul regularly with bright, warm thoughts and feelings … Thoughts are transported between souls through waves … We have free will, we can make our own choices, but you have to know what is right and wrong.

God has given us light, an electric fire, to serve our will … The world is magnetized by light, which is also called astral light or starlight. It has a dual movement of attraction and repulsion. We are attracted and attract, we repel and are repelled … Fools are more sensitive to magnetism than people with common sense …

There was a chapter on "Magic, Dreams, Mysteries, and Omens."

What follows is advice on how you can protect yourself from evil eyes and ill will. How you can find peace and inner happiness ... Use a red bracelet ... You can be enchanted by radiation, looks, contact, words ... You can kill with magic just as with electricity ... Do not believe in fortunes that speak of something bad.

In the last chapter, dedicated to Flora and her son, Jasha, were accounts of their ancestry, family members, and what they did, as well as a list of family members who were killed in concentration camps during World War II.

On the last page, Tilda wrote:

To Flora:
Family secrets:
Two curses plague our family because of something that happened two generations ago. I have had one removed. The second curse means that we are affected by certain diseases. Find the right person to neutralize the curse and bring about balance in the family. Maybe a rabbi or some other respected person can help. Note signs in your dreams or visions. You can also talk to a fortune teller who is not out to trick you. But remember, if you decide to do so, she must not be sick, neither in body nor soul. And she must wash hands and bless

both you and her. If she does not follow this advice, it can have unfortunate consequences. I knew a fortune teller but at some point, she turned bad and did things associated with witchcraft. I helped her and freed her from the evil.

You can also try to remove the curse yourself. You will find the instructions on page 61. You will need certain prayers. They are on page 63. I have been told that if you do not succeed, the responsibility rests on Jasha and his children. One of them will remove the curse effortlessly … I can see it.

Do not open the book until I am dead, and if someone else does open it, they must ask for forgiveness.

40

TRANSFORMATION
SARAJEVO, DECEMBER 13, 1996

Today is two months since I started working in the kindergarten. I feel like I've always belonged there. The rooms exude freshness with newly painted walls and used but nice furniture that we, the staff, brought from home or collected from neighbors, friends, and acquaintances, along with toys and plants.

The children who have lost one or both parents seem content to have some adults who pay attention to them, praise them, and show them how to behave in the big world. They mostly look up to Jakob, who was hired recently, and who makes them jump and dance when he sings and plays the guitar.

I told Jakob he doesn't need to keep searching for a piece of paper or anything else from Sara's grandmother, Tilda, or Flora. That it doesn't matter to me anymore.

I told him this at six in the morning. He was startled when I called, but I apologized for the early hour. He was already up, he said.

Before then I had woken with a clear-cut decision

that I should reject omens and fortunes. Without getting angry.

It was as if I'd had an epiphany. Like I'd come back to myself. But I was also saddened by the fact that the time before the war will never return.

I packed Tilda's book, wrote Jasha's address on the package, and headed to the post office.

41

Twilight ... My eyes are dazzled ... And open.

There stands Tilda all in white. Her face is radiant. I ask what she wants.

She disappears. Smiling. It feels like it's the very last time I shall see her spirit.

***

The evening has long since unfolded its capricious side. There is something magical, something inexplicable about the light, tingling air. A great tit in the garden insists on being heard at the late hour.

I lie in bed, relaxing. Suddenly there's a knock on the door. It makes me jump. A voice from the hallway asks, "Masha, are you home?"

"Who is it?"

"An old friend. Will you open the door?"

I open the door. Can't believe my eyes and stammer, "But ... you were ... killed ... in the hospital!"

"I was. But only for a few hours. I was clinically

dead. When I woke up I found myself in a coffin, but an orderly heard my cries. I've been looking for you. And now you are here. In front of me! It's hard to believe. Elvira died recently in Canada. A friend learned I was alive and sent me her diary where she wrote about you and ... I have a lot to tell you."

"So have I ... and ... *this* is yours. I took it from you when you finished your military service. I've been looking after it all these years."

***

Author's note:
The song "Adio Kerida" mentioned in the book
is on the author's website: narcisavucina.dk.
It's in English except the refrain, which is in Ladino.

Sinéad Quirke Køngerskov, PhD, is an award-winning Danish to English translator. In 2022, her translation of *Coffee, Rabbit, Snowdrop, Lost* by Betina Birkjær and Anna Margrethe Kjærgaard (Enchanted Lion) received a Batchelder Honor Award, was listed as a USBBY Outstanding International Book and was announced as a Kirkus Prize 2022 finalist. Sinéad is secretary of DELT (the Association of Danish to English Literary Translators) and was SmokeLong Quarterly's guest editor for Danish. She lives in Denmark with her husband and son and their three cats. You can read more about her at folkvangengelsk.com

Narcisa Vucina was born in multi-ethnic Sarajevo, Bosnia and Herzegovina. She lives in Copenhagen, Denmark, where she married a Dane. She holds a Masters in English, University of Sarajevo; exam. Art. in Slavic languages, University of Copenhagen; studied English Language and British Literature at Cambridge College, London; took lessons in American English at the Hollywood Work Source; studied Italian and some other languages; speaks Swedish. The languages she writes in are Danish, English and Croatian/Bosnian. Narcisa was trained in journalism at the Danish Broadcasting Corporation, DR; full-time journalist/News Reporter at the Danish Broadcasting Corporation; freelancer for *Politiken* and other newspapers. In her journalistic work, culture had an important role. She interviewed, among others, David Bowie, Joseph Brodsky, David Lynch, *Les Compagnons de la Chanson* (Edit Piaf's vocal group). Some of her articles are about The Sarajevo Haggadah, the first female rabbi in Central and Eastern Europe, and ghosts in a Danish castle. Vucina was hired by the University of Copenhagen to teach Bosnian/ Croatian/Serbian, which she did for twenty-two years.

www.ingramcontent.com/pod-product-compliance
Lightning Source LLC
Chambersburg PA
CBHW011150310726
48973CB00010B/2846